Destination Unknown

A Desperate Tale Of Survival

Larry Dodson

ISBN-13: 978-1508488705

Destination Unknown

Copyright © 2015 by Larry Dodson

All rights reserved. Accept for use in any review, the reproduction or utilization of this work in whole or in part in any form by any electronic, mechanical or other means, now known or hereafter invented including xerography, photocopying and recording, or in any information storage or retrieval system, is forbidden without the written permission of the publisher. Larry J. Dodson, 520 7th Street W #951, Palmetto, FL 34220

All characters in this book have no existence outside the imagination of the author and have no relation whatsoever to anyone bearing the same name or names. They are not even distantly inspired by any individual known or unknown to the author, and all incidents are pure invention.

Dedicated to my wife Kacy, without her encouragement and loving support this book would have not been possible.

Chapter 1

On The Eve...

Brandon woke to the annoying whistle of the six-thirty freight train making its daily run to the local fruit juice plant. What started out as another balmy October morning would end up changing life as he and his wife Judy had grown accustomed to.

Brandon and Judy chose to spend their retirement years living on a small sailboat. They enjoy being tethered to civilization by living in a marina that provides them with most of the amenities people on shore take for granted. The marina they chose to live in came fully stocked with all the colorful characters you would expect by living in what Brandon jokingly refers to as a floating trailer park. Their liveaboard sailing neighbors provided an endless supply of knowledge, insight, enlightenment and gossip.

The decision to retire on a sailboat was easy. They believed a well-equipped sailboat represented the ultimate bug-out vehicle, or more specifically, "bug- out vessel". Sailboats were self-contained, mobile and could adequately carry the needed provisions to sustain life as well as provide an easy way to distance themselves in the event of civil unrest.

Both were of the belief it was just a matter of time before SHTF.

The couple had started making preparations to provision "Sparrow", a small full keel cutter rig ketch two years earlier. They had acquired what they considered absolute must have items to be truly self-sufficient. Relocating Sparrow from the cold California coastline to the warm Florida waters was at the top of the list. They figured their survival in the event of a national catastrophe would be greatly increased by moving to a warmer climate, an abundance of fish, and the ability to capture rainwater, three of the main ingredients required for self-sufficient survival. Their decision to relocate to a marina in Palmetto was based solely on the historical lack of hurricane activity over the past eighty years.

The town of Palmetto lies approximately five miles up the Manatee River which flowed into Tampa Bay. The much larger city of Bradenton is situated directly across the river connected by a four lane concrete bridge about a mile long.

After living in the hustle-bustle congestion of the San Francisco Bay area the last five years, moving to the small town atmosphere of Palmetto was a welcome treat. As a boater this was as close to heaven as it gets.

Careful thought had gone into upgrading Sparrow's seaworthiness and self-sufficiency. New sails, electric motor, dinghy, three month's worth of food for two and a manual salt water desalinator would prove invaluable should a national crisis arise. Phase one took little over a year to acquire all the necessary supplies to survive without outside assistance. Phase two entailed saving enough money to have Sparrow trucked to Florida with enough funds left over to comfortably re-establish their lives.

One thing Brandon and Judy had come to realize, they enjoyed socializing with their neighbors, but in the event of a national emergency people were going to be the first thing to avoid. Most boaters, like the general population, only maintain about three days' worth of food and Sparrow would be stocked like a floating convenience store. One advantage Sparrow possessed was her unassuming small size compared to larger "yacht" looking boats. Odds were in her favor she would be ignored as just another small boat looking for a handout. At least that was their hope. Still, avoidance at all cost was essential at least until things eventually settled into what they would be.

Brandon went about his typical morning routine turning on the TV and tuning to his favorite news/talk station. Judy started a pot of coffee. Nothing of any notoriety to report, stock market up, some report of yet another country the U. S. was having political problems with...same old same old. After fifteen minutes the decision was made to switch to watching "I Love Lucy" before taking care of their daily chores. Brandon took his coffee out the companionway to enjoy a cigarette in the open air of the cockpit. The faint sound of the busy road about twelve hundred feet away buzzed with light steady traffic as the morning commute got underway.

Judy popped her head out of the companionway to let Brandon know, "The cable box isn't working for some reason."

Brandon knew that was code for "fix the TV." "I'll take a look at it in a minute" he said as he continued to smoke.

The buzzing trance of the traffic was suddenly interrupted by squealing tires and the sound of a multiple car crash. Brandon strained to see the direction of the noise hidden just out of view by trees.

"Whoa, did you hear that? I think someone must have run the signal light."

Judy entered the cockpit scanning the same direction Brandon was facing. Unable to catch a glimpse she mumbled, "I'm glad we don't have to deal with rush hour anymore."

Brandon shook his head in agreement. "I'll take a look at what's wrong with the TV. Maybe they'll have something on the news later."

Brandon was fairly good at systematic problem solving. A few minutes later he reported his findings to Judy.

"The TV is working fine. It's getting plenty of power from the batteries."

"What about the cable?"

"Cables plugged in. For some reason it just doesn't want to pick up any stations. If it keeps up, you'll have to call the cable company to find out what's wrong."

"Turn on the radio, see if it works."

As Brandon started to comment "What does that gotta do with the TV... "He stopped short as he realized her request suggested the possibility that the wreck and the TV might have originated from the same event.

A few seconds later Brandon informed her "Nothing but static on all of the stations."

Judy took on a puzzled look as she responded, "Some of the stations are over forty miles away. I have a feeling it must be more than a local problem."

Without so much as a second thought, she went below deck, rummaging through the compartments in the v-berth to find Sparrow's "ditch bag", moments later pulling out a battery powered portable shortwave radio. Though the radio couldn't transmit, it was capable of listening to shortwave communications around the world. Brandon plugged a long wire into the radio which functioned as the antenna as per the multi-lingual instructions.

Judy subconsciously started nervously twisting the ends of her long brown hair as Brandon glossed over the instructions one more time. Satisfied that everything was in order he flipped the switch on.

The small contraption sprang to life emitting whining sounds which Brandon eventually fine-tuned to receive what sounded like two women talking about dating. As their voices drifted in and out of coherency it was obvious they were as clueless as Brandon and Judy as to what was happening in Central Florida. As he continued turning the knob, he briefly caught on to another conversation that drifted off into static.

"The instructions say the signal will vary with the time of day, something about bouncing the signal off the atmosphere. I'll try again in an hour or so."

Brandon gave a confident smile to Judy. She didn't return a look of confidence in the small radio.

The two sat in the cockpit discussing the long term consequences of a statewide blackout and mutually agreed to start preparing Sparrow for cruising just in case the situation spun out of control.

They figured there was no need to panic and they had enough time to ready the boat without drawing unwanted attention. Having spent the last six years living in a marina they knew someone was always watching what you do.

Judy uncoiled the hose on the dock to begin topping off Sparrows water tank while Brandon disconnected the now useless power cord.

The decision was made two years earlier to install an electric inboard motor in Sparrow as opposed to replacing her undependable diesel. Scarcity of fuel in the event of a nationwide calamity clinched the decision to go electric. The electric motor had its disadvantages when it came to continuous run time, but proved more than adequate for going in and out of anchorages. An additional solar panel was dedicated to charging the motor away from the dock, freeing them of the need for dockside a/c power and unwanted contact with people.

As preparations covertly progressed on the boat, car horns as well as the distinct sound of emergency sirens started to increase throughout the surrounding neighborhood. Something extraordinary was taking place.

"Judy, come check this out."

As Judy stepped out into the cockpit three military helicopters flying in close formation flew over the marina headed in the direction of Tampa Bay. "You don't see that every day!"

The thunderous roar of the helicopter engines briefly drowned out the sound of a community on the threshold of collapse.

In retrospect, the horns and sirens expressed frustration, something you could relate to. Frustration would soon be giving way to panic when the chaotic noise ceased. The lack of sirens would reflect the collapse of local governmental control over the masses and ultimately end with the pillaging of the haves, by the have nots.

Brandon tried to ease the moment, "Let's not get panicky and freak out."

"OK sweetie, but if things are still screwed up tomorrow, I want to leave."

Brandon and Judy, like most Americans, had grown up in a nanny society of abundance. If you couldn't acquire the basic needs, the government would provide it for you. They never had to fear starvation or a roof over their head. For the first time in their lives there was no assurance of anything. Staying alive in the near future could be dependent on new, yet to be learned survival skills and the ability to adapt on the fly. The only light at the end of the tunnel came in the form of staying alive long enough to rejoin a fledgling society somewhere down the road. They suddenly realized their lives as well as the rest of the country might never be the same.

As they lay in bed that night listening to sporadic unfamiliar noises emanating from the little town just beyond the marina, they questioned if all the time and effort they put into preparing themselves for living in a world without order. Probably not, but only time would tell.

Chapter 2

Time to Leave

A few hours after day break on the second day, Richard, a boating neighbor stood on the finger pier alongside Sparrow. "Judy, Brandon, anybody on board?" which was the customary way of announcing yourself in an environment lacking front doors and door bells.

"Yeah, be right out." Brandon knew Richard was keenly aware of what was transpiring and one of the few boaters who routinely bragged about hoarding six months' worth of food for just such an event that was appearing to unfold.

As Brandon exited the cabin Richard quietly inquired, "What's your take on the power outage?" Richard's tone expressed an uncertainty which ran contrary to his usual confident "I always know what's going on attitude."

"We don't know for sure. We've been trying to pick up shortwave radio signals but haven't had any luck. We should have spent a little more money on a more reliable radio."

"I haven't heard anything either, but I did hear what sounded like automatic gunfire last night and I don't think it was the cops. I'm seriously thinking about getting out of dodge while I can. I mean like, how long before looters end up in the marina?"

Without conferring with Judy, Brandon casually asked, "Want Company?" He assumed that was why Richard was there.

"You bet. If nothing comes of it, we'll still have a good time cruising. I've talked to two other boats that want to join in, you know, a safety in numbers thing."

"Who else is going?"

Richard paused for a moment, "Mark, Luann, and George with the Islander 32."

Brandon and Judy considered Mark and LuAnn a down to earth couple with great personalities. Mark had a good sense of humor and LuAnn an infectious smile. On more than one occasion the couples had discussed sailboats being the "ultimate survival vehicle", or in this case, "vessel" in the event things went south with the government.

"I don't know George. How well do you know him?"

"Well, he seems pretty normal to me. He owns a shit load of guns."

Brandon thought to himself another with weapons would be an excellent addition, that is, as long as the small armada of fleeing boats pulled together as a team. Besides, this was Richard's parade. Brandon had an opportunity to either join, or strike out alone.

"Sounds good, when are you planning on leaving?"

"I'll let you know within the hour." He stepped off the boat onto the dock. "Hang loose."

Brandon impatiently waited for Judy to return to the boat. She had left just prior to Richard's visit to take advantage of the marina's shower facilities. Both had figured it would only be a short time before the water in the large above-ground storage tank would empty as it required electricity to run the pumps. He was excited and a little nervous as the gravity of what was about to happen had morphed from what if, to what now. This wasn't a game this was real life. Brandon was confident she would agree on the decision to join Richard and the other two boats.

Upon Judy's return Brandon informed her of Richard's plan. As the two discussed the positive aspects of a group departure they started jotting down questions they would ask Richard at the upcoming meeting. They also wrote down a few suggestions they would bounce off the other boaters in hopes of developing a sustainable strategy. There was nothing left to do but wait for Richard.

Forty minutes had passed before Richard returned with the message they were all going to meet on his boat at eleven o'clock. Once again a sense of excitement started to build in Brandon as he realized they might not be able to control what was going on beyond the marina, but the open water would at least provide them the opportunity to somewhat control their destiny.

The idea of looters invading the marina, having to defend your food supply or worse, being rounded up and sent to live in a FEMA camp reinforced the decision to leave.

Entering Richard's boat, they couldn't help but pick up on the somber atmosphere of the meeting. Mark, Luann, George and Richard shifted positions around the small table to make room for Brandon and Judy. Richard's seventeen-year-old daughter Amanda, sat cross legged on the floor a few feet from the group.

Richard opened with, "Any ideas?"

Everyone took a turn making suggestions, some good, some summarily dismissed. What struck Brandon was the confident no nonsense attitude of the attendees. This was a group that would not tolerate weak insecure personalities that would end up hampering their escape. Richard had succeeded in assembling like-minded self-reliant sailors. You just knew if you couldn't pull your own weight you'd be cut loose.

The group carefully examined a chart of the area. They agreed to rendezvous at 27 degrees, 22.25 North, by 83 degrees 21.9 West. A position located 35 miles offshore. The total distance to reach their destination would require sailing a total of 47 nautical miles and under normal conditions take about eight hours to reach. The offshore location would give them the opportunity to take their time in deciding their next move.

Richard went on to suggest all radar reflectors be removed and absolutely no running lights displayed at any time. VHF radio communication would be restricted to being within eye contact of another boat, and then only on low power settings. Ironically, the weakness with VHF radios has always been its short line of sight range of five to fifteen miles, but in their current situation the short distance would become an asset in keeping their position silent from prying ears.

The final decision of when to leave was set for eight-thirty that evening. They planned on the darkness minimizing their detection on the river. The small fleet would stagger their departures as not to draw unwanted attention. The marina they lived in sat approximately five miles up the Manatee River. Once clearing the river, they would have to sail eleven more miles to cross Tampa Bay in order to reach the Gulf of Mexico. If there was going to be a problem the trip down the one-mile wide river would be it. The multi-million dollar homes that lined both sides of the banks would soon be stripped of their treasures by bands of opportunistic looters. What Brandon feared most was gun wielding whackos taking their frustration out on passing boats. Brandon knew clearing the river and entering the Gulf would sever their invisible umbilical cord with a society gone wild.

The meeting came to an end. The usual small talk from the group ended as well. They knew there would be plenty of time for that bobbing out at sea.

Chapter 3

Departure

Brandon and Judy couldn't help but notice the increase in foot traffic meandering around the marina. If this had been the weekend it would have gone unnoticed but today was Thursday. It soon became apparent many of the boat owners were prepping their boats for extended cruising. It wasn't unusual to see people filling their water tanks, it was however out of place to see them filling up multiple five-gallon jerry cans, including anything that could carry additional water.

Word started circulating from person to person of the widespread panic in the world just outside of the marina. Accounts of desperate people trying to gather supplies to feed their families as well as buying anything they could find to repel potential looters. The total absence of civil authorities to protect life, as well as property, did not paint a pretty picture. The official rumor was the calamity appeared to be nationwide, but in the new world of word-of-mouth information ran the risk of containing more speculation than fact.

As the afternoon wore on, additional horror stories began to circulate around the marina. Firsthand accounts of lifeless bodies strewn on front entry-ways and lawns shed no clues as to whether they were the victims or the perpetrators. Markets with shattered windows recently liberated of everything edible. People breaking into hardware stores to fortify personal property and numerous fires most likely set out of frustration. It became obvious it wouldn't be long before the waterfront would be invaded next.

As darkness fell upon the landscape it was Brandon and Judy's turn to leave the marina. Brandon prepared to cast off Sparrow's dock lines for the last time. The black plumes of smoke that dotted the horizon during the day now took on an eerie orange and yellow cast. Sporadic gunfire intensified as orderly civilization continued to collapse. A couple of dozen boats had left the marina that day and now it was their turn.

Shortly after purchasing Sparrow two years earlier Brandon and Judy decided who would do what in order to sail Sparrow as efficiently as possible. Judy would do the helming and take care of her small mizzen sail. Brandon would handle the two working jibs, mainsail, anchoring and any other foredeck duties including casting off. Judy's excellent eyesight along with her keen interest in channel markers freed Brandon to do what he enjoyed most, keeping the sails trimmed and, according to Brandon, avoiding the monotony of steering.

As Sparrow eased out of her slip, Judy pushed the throttle down as the silent electric motor slowly gained momentum. This is going to be interesting, Brandon thought, as Judy negotiated the last turn out of the marina for the open river. Motoring five miles against the current to clear the river would deplete most of Sparrow's battery power but would not present a long term problem. They could use their solar panel to recharge the batteries the next day. Sailing on the other hand would save her batteries but would take considerably longer to reach the Gulf. How long did they want to spend traversing the river with all the potential threats from both banks? The decision to motor seemed the safer choice of the two.

As Judy carefully avoided numerous sandbars in the river, Brandon scanned the once well-lit west bank for signs of life. So strange to see the large mansions unlit and vulnerable. No fires, no shots, no nothing. Brandon considered it a good sign as the boat silently made way.

Suddenly his thoughts were interrupted as Judy broke the silence.

"There's a boat coming up fast with no lights on."

It was obvious the boat was trying not to draw unwanted attention. It might have had its running lights off but the sound of its powerful motor could be heard for some distance. The problem they faced was Sparrow wasn't running her lights as well. The boat was speeding toward Sparrows stern at a high rate of speed.

Brandon yelled to Judy "We've got no choice. I've got to turn on the lights."

Within seconds Brandon had managed to enter the cabin and turn on the running light switch.

"It's still holding course!" Judy hollered.

For the next few seconds they feared the journey would end in a collision on the river. The instant illumination of an object dead ahead had successfully warned the speeding boat to steer clear as it altered course just enough to pass Sparrow on her port side.

"Did you see that? The boat must have had twenty people on board."

Judy didn't reply as she maintained control of Sparrow as she violently rocked from the enormous bow wake thrown off from the passing boat. Brandon went below and turned the lights off.

The next few minutes were spent in silence as they neared the halfway point. Brandon not knowing if Judy was speaking to him or to herself whispered, "So far, so good."

The next section of the river was much wider and with Sparrow's shallow draft of three and a half feet would give them plenty of sea room to dance around any errant boats fleeing in the dark. Ten minutes later Judy again whispered, "Approaching Desoto Point."

The popular anchorage was empty.

"No one on the hook. I guess that would make sense. Only an idiot would anchor close enough for someone to throw a Molotov cocktail at your boat."

For some reason Brandon found his statement humorous as he let out a slight chuckle.

The wind was blowing out of the northeast at around 12 knots. As Sparrow's batteries were drawing down on power it was time to continue the escape by raising sails. Thanks to twin roller furlers Brandon did not have to leave the cockpit to raise both jibs. Loosening her furler lines he easily pulled on the port side jib sheets allowing both sails to fill with air. Judy pulled on the mizzen halyard to raise the small sail up. As she tied off the halyard she quickly trimmed the small sail as Sparrow silently moved through the water. The decision to raise the mainsail would be delayed until they reached the open waters of the Gulf of Mexico.

The final challenge to reach the open water of the Gulf would be sailing between Passage Key and Egmont Key, two relatively small islands separated by a narrow channel. Passage Key resembled a large above water sandbar and Egmont Key once maintained a fort to protect Tampa Bay. The fort had been decommissioned years ago and the only full time resident on the island was a Park Ranger.

"Hope the Ranger got off the Island." Brandon said, knowing it would be very easy to reach by scavenging small boats.

Reaching the north end of Egmont Key Judy prepared to tack Sparrow. She kept clear of the dangerous sandy shoals. This would not be a place to be stuck on a sandbar. As Judy eased the tiller to change direction they were startled to see the red embers of a burnt out shell of a boat just managing to barely stay afloat. The calmness that Judy and Brandon had slipped into was instantly replaced by the sudden adrenalin rush brought on by the presence of the still smoldering wreckage.

"This couldn't have happened more than a few hours ago." Judy said as she feverishly scanned the darkness for any signs of trouble.

"Yeah, I wonder if it was over fuel." Brandon also adding, "Boats that size can carry a couple of hundred gallons. Imagine getting killed over gasoline, what a trip."

Whatever the reason, Brandon and Judy had witnessed firsthand the harsh reality and need for constant vigilance in a changing world.

Brandon let out a deep breath, looked over in Judy's direction and whispered, "Well Judy, welcome to the world of Mad Max."

Chapter 4

Rendezvous

Sparrow made her way through the small northeast swells with rhythmic grace as she distanced a darkening shoreline. The only remaining sign of civilization along the coast came in the form of yellow and orange fires from burning homes that once represented comfort and relative safety. Those lucky enough to enjoy living in a house with an ocean view now found themselves trapped between encroaching chaos and the sea.

As Brandon adjusted sails to compensate for a minor wind shift Judy maintained a steady course through the dark. She carefully monitored the electronic chart plotter for direction, one of the few systems not dependent on grid power.

"If the plotter ever goes down were going to have to rely on your celestial navigation skills."

"Yeah" Brandon replied," the trouble with that is it only takes seconds for the GPS to find our position, and that's pinning it down to thirty feet. It's going to take me about thirty minutes to take two sights, compute a fix, and then all we can hope for is accuracy of two to five miles, so enjoy the chart plotter while it still works."

Judy thought to herself, two to five miles was still better than not having a clue.

Normally sailing at night they would stand two hour watches. One would rest or sleep, the other control the helm and keep an eye on the sails. This wasn't going to happen tonight as there was nothing normal about this voyage. Tonight required all eyes on deck until they reached the rendezvous point.

Brandon took the helm so Judy could go below to fix something for them to eat. Sparrow carried enough provisions to easily feed them for a couple of months. Brandon and Judy usually snacked while they were sailing and saved the more time consuming meals for anchorages.

Cooking and eating underway required skills usually reserved for circus balancing acts. You end up with more food in your lap than in your stomach. A few minutes later she returned with fruit, salami, cheese and crackers.

"Excellent" replied Brandon "He knew they only carried a small amount of perishable food which they would have to eat before it went bad, after that it would be Spam City. Lucky for them they had acquired a liking for Spam as Brandon like to joke, "cook mine medium rare." With over eighty cans onboard its popularity was sure to be short lived. The smell and taste of steak and pork chops would only be consumed in their dreams.

In addition to Spam, Sparrow housed a full array of canned goods, hot cocoa, dried fruits, peanut butter and so on. A large bag of rice, pancake mix and other "add water" supplies would only be enjoyed with an adequate supply of water. Though Sparrow only carried thirty gallons of fresh water an additional eleven gallons could be supplemented from her separate fresh water cockpit shower in a pinch. Barring a lapse in capturing rainwater she also carried a manual saltwater desalinator as a last resort. Brandon had pretested the water maker and had come to the conclusion it took so much physical energy to produce so little water the best thing they could do was "pray for rain".

The miles slipped by as they continued scanning the horizon for other boats. On one hand it would be comforting to catch sight of one of the other three boats in their group, but on the other hand, crossing paths with strangers could end up with lethal results.

Brandon estimated they would rejoin the group in approximately four hours as long as the sailing conditions remained unchanged. Without running lights, getting within visual distance without running into each other could prove dicey in the dark. The worst case scenario of a collision with another boat would be eliminated by waiting until daybreak. The ultimate worst case scenario still remained not finding them at all.

Forty minutes later Judy spotted something out of place some distance off of Sparrow's port side. With the aid of binoculars, she was barely able to distinguish the distinct shape of a sailboat. The boat was sailing a parallel course, maintaining the same speed and no visible running lights. Was it one of their group? Should they set an evasive course to starboard? They had to decide something fast and in this case fast meant slow, slow Sparrow down. If the unknown boat continued to hold course it could only mean one of two things, (A) it was a member of their group heading for the rendezvous coordinates or (B) they were being paced by the other boat.

As Sparrow slowed due to Brandon easing the sheets, it soon became apparent the unknown boat was continuing to maintain course and speed. Odds were in their favor it was one of their allies. As the boat became undiscernible in the dark Brandon once again tightened up the sheets in order to resume their previous speed and heading. With tensions easing Judy and Brandon took refuge in the thought that at least one of their group could possibly be waiting to greet them at the rendezvous point.

Judy, reflecting on yesterday's meeting, brought up how hard this was going to be on

Richard. His wife had died a couple of years back from breast cancer. Raising a daughter all alone would have been tough enough, but now he had to protect her from a volatile unknown future in a violent environment. Both agreed they were spared his frustration with their son actively serving in the Air Force. Whatever lay ahead, at least their son would fall under the protection of the military. Their only concern was how to reunite with him when the country reformed.

Ten hours had passed since leaving port. The darkness gave way to twilight as the faint features of a barren landscape began to appear.

Judy, scanning the area ahead of them, turned to Brandon, "Shouldn't we be seeing the other boats by now?"

"Well, they say you can see about fifteen miles to the horizon, but with this slight haze I wouldn't count on it. According to the GPS we have about six miles to go."

As they both scanned the horizon Judy broke the suspense. "I think I see something to starboard at our two o'clock. It looks like a couple of boats. What do you think?"

After a few seconds Brandon confirmed her sighting. "Yeah, I see it too. I'll use the radio when we get a little closer."

A sense of relief settled over Brandon and Judy as she maneuvered Sparrow toward the bobbing boats. It appeared Richard, George and Mark had all arrived unscathed.

During the course of the marina meeting they talked about keeping their identities secret over the radio.

Richard was assigned #1. Mark and LuAnn #2. George #3 and Brandon and Judy #4.

The reason behind concealing their identities over the radio was to lessen the chance of unscrupulous ears ease dropping on the identity of a particular boat discussing matters of food or weaponry.

As Sparrow sailed within a quarter mile of the group Brandon picked up the mike and announced, "Number 4, present and accounted for. Walk in the park."

Chapter 5

Surprise!

Brandon and Judy's elation with rejoining the group came to an abrupt halt as Richard announced over the radio, "By the way, George brought two friends to join us."

Brandon could sense Richard's statement echoed a slight pensive tone. Red flags were instantly flying at full staff.

Judy turned to Brandon speaking in a low voice, "Great, we don't even know that much about George and now he's taken on two more people. How much food could he possibly carry on his boat? What's going to happen if he runs out? I think its bullshit he didn't say a word about them at the meeting."

Brandon whole heartedly shared Judy's sentiment adding. "Yeah, it looks like Mr. Gunboat just became Mr. Gunship!"

Richard continued his announcement, "The water is a little too rough right now to raft up, everyone stay within eyesight of each other. Report anything you see on the water. Number 1 out."

Casually panning the horizon with binoculars Judy could see Amanda sitting near the helm of Richard's boat. She couldn't tell who was sitting in the cockpit of Marks boat so she nonchalantly turned her attention to George's crew. She could clearly make out the distinct shape of three men onboard.

"I don't like this at all. One of his crew looks like a thin man wearing a large straw hat and the other has a husky build. No I take that back, he's just fat."

Brandon knew the addition of two more mouths to feed would strain what food resources the convoy carried. The group could possibly stretch their supplies by fishing, and in shallow enough waters try to catch lobster. Fish or not, Brandon knew when the food runs out it was going to be the beginning of yet another potentially lethal learning experience.

Not one to jinx a situation, Brandon looking off to the horizon turned to Judy as he said, "Let's just think positive, try to get along and be ready to split if things don't work out."

Judy smiled as she thought "Which part was positive, getting along, or the getting away part?"

Brandon also brought up the fact "Who knows, maybe more people carrying guns could give them additional protection, create a sort of scare factor."

Judy lowered the binoculars. "OK, I'll go in with an open mind, but they're still guilty until proven otherwise."

They both laughed as she returned to scanning the horizon.

Brandon and Judy were great at the "what if" game, but feeling exhausted from the overnighter they decided talk of George and his crew could wait until tomorrow.

Around four o'clock the radio silence was broken with, "This is number 2 the water is starting to flatten. What do you guys think about rafting up for a few hours, over?"

Mark was right, the sea had calmed down. "This is number 1, I'm in."

Followed shortly with George and Brandon agreeing as well.

"This will give us a chance to see what George's buddies are like." Brandon quipped as he placed the protective fenders along Sparrow's starboard side. Being the smallest boat in their fleet, Judy requested tying Sparrow up alongside Mark's portside. She also radioed a request for an end tie. It would not be comfortable seeing Sparrow squashed between two larger boats, and this would give Brandon and Judy an excuse not to tie up alongside George, upon whom the jury was still out.

After securely tying Sparrow off, Brandon and Judy boarded Mark and LuAnn's boat. The two couples exchanged genuine hugs and smiles. Any signs of nervousness were carefully concealed to promote confidence and boost group morale.

Uncertainties would be subject to group discussions at a later date.

The two couples helped tie off Richard's boat to Mark's starboard side, then rendered assistance to George, who also elected to have an end tie. George was first to climb aboard, closely followed by his newly acquired crewmen.

"This is Mike, and this is Jordan. These guys have never sailed but they've got the right attitude."

No one responded to George's comment as the group slowly selected a comfortable place to sit on Richard's boat.

Judy took the opportunity to take mental notes of George and his crew. George looked to be in his early thirties. He seemed to exhibit an air of contempt for any ideas other than his own. His short height of 5' 8" probably played a role in his overly aggressive attitude. Jordan appeared the exact opposite. Late teens or early twenties, the thin man was quiet and appeared respectful. If there was a rebellious bone in his body, it came in the form of having one too many tattoos on his arms. Mike, now there was a challenge.

Overweight and unkempt, you just knew he didn't give a shit about anyone or anything. He wasn't the least bit interested in what was going on.

The next couple of hours passed quickly as the group discussed plans to relocate to an island somewhere in the Exuma out island chain. They agreed to consult the charts on their individual boats and make a group decision the next day. As they shifted to more relaxed subjects Brandon pulled a cigarette from his pack and lit up.

"Hey, you got a spare smoke?"

It was Mike.

Brandon came back with his favorite response, "Never bought a pack with spares, do they attach them to the outside of the pack?"

As the group chuckled you could see Mike starting to turn pinkish red.

"Hey Dude, I thought George said this was a share and share alike thing."

Brandon didn't like Mikes tone, let alone his message.

"Listen my friend, I was just kidding, I don't mind giving you a cigarette, but they're not community property. You did bring your own smokes didn't you?"

You could see Mike's face turning different shades of red.

"Fuck you. Fuck you and your cigarettes."

He abruptly stood up and stormed back to George's boat. George made no excuse for Mike's over the top temper tantrum. George and Jordan casually got up and left as well. George parting with, "I can see you two are going to get along just peachy."

Waiting until George and his friends went below deck everyone tightened the circle. Mark wanted to know what would give George, or his crew any indication everything was going to be split evenly among the group. No one actually knew how much food or fuel was carried on each boat. It wouldn't be right to penalize the one who provisioned their boat with an abundance of food and supplies and expect him to share with piggy's who carelessly set out with nothing more than "attitude".

You never wanted to reveal exactly everything you carried to anyone. Richard, they assumed, would only invite people that had mentioned stowing a couple of months' worth of supplies on onboard. It was looking like George had slipped through the cracks and saw the group as a way to make up for his lack of preparation.

Everyone knew deep down, as harsh as it would appear, when you ran out of food you'd be expected to voluntarily leave the group. The small convoy really only amounted to little more than moral support. No assurances were ever made as to sharing food or supplies.

The next two or three weeks would reveal whether George should remain, or be cast from the group.

As the rest of the members began to leave for their boats you could sense the feeling of "what have we gotten ourselves into". It was assumed Richard would unofficially lead the group. Throughout the evening's meeting George constantly suggested he should lead instead of Richard based on his ability to best protect the boats. His proposal felt more like a mafia protection threat than looking out for their best interests. Sticking with the group could prove as fatal as staying in the marina if George were to get out of control.

Lying on her bunk, Judy reached over to turn off the interior light.

Brandon, reflecting on the evenings events mused,

"Who would have thought a cigarette could be the harbinger of things to come."

Chapter 6

Exit Strategy

Brandon and Judy were early risers. They woke well before sunrise. They capitalized on being the downwind boat to hide the distinct smell of frying bacon. From this point on hiding food smells escaping Sparrow's small galley would be of paramount importance, only followed by stealthily disposing of empty cans and food wrappers. Both realized there would be occasions when a can of beef stew would have to be consumed cold to avoid its distinct aroma.

Shortly after eating, Brandon dove overboard to enjoy a refreshing dip in the warm gulf water. Besides feeling cleaner, the sea water would also wash away any lingering food odors. Granted, the salt water would tend to mat Brandon's hair but found the dry salt water on his skin not all that uncomfortable.

Judy motioned him over to the side of the boat. "They're ready to start the meeting."

"Tell them I'll be right there", as he swam toward the swim ladder.

Brandon and Judy had decided before going to bed to let the island selection be made by the larger boats. With Sparrow's shallow three-and-a-half-foot draft, she could easily anchor anywhere they chose. Besides, they had just recently arrived from California and had no experience in Bahamian waters.

As Richard and Mark went over a large paper chart, George appeared unconcerned. Like Judy and Brandon, he had resolved to let someone else pick the destination. With over a thousand islands to choose from, the only criterion ended up being an island uninhabited and having adequate depth to anchor in.

Richard happened to notice Jordan staring at Amanda. It was obvious Jordan was attracted to his teenage daughter. Amanda was a petite, thin figured attractive young women. Under different circumstances she could have easily landed a modeling career when she finished high school.

Jordan was oblivious to Richard's smirk as he returned to the chart. Evidently Jordan didn't fit Richard's criteria as a potential suitor for his daughter. The decision was made. Richard turned to face everyone while Mark started to write the coordinates on small slips of paper. Richard, in a voice lacking emotion, informed the group the island was located approximately eight hundred nautical miles from their present position. Richard and Mark also decided to make a judgment call on whether or not to make a quick stop over at the Dry Tortuga's should the weather threaten their journey. He went on to say, sailing at a minimum of four knots would take them about twelve days.

Jordan was to first to speak, "Why so long, shouldn't it take about five days?"

Richard explained to the newbie "It could in a power boat, but sailboats rarely sail a straight line. We have to factor in wind direction and adverse conditions. Believe me, I've sailed there more than a dozen times, twelve days is a realistic estimate."

"Bummer", replied Jordan, "Give me a power boat any day."

No one felt like taking the time to explain the merits of using the wind to move as opposed to a future of non-existent fuel supplies.

Richard continued, "We should try to stay together. Use the radio sparingly and whatever you do don't broadcast your position, or our destination. Keep your eyes peeled for other boats and don't lose sight of one another."

George interrupted Richard, "No problem, I'm not going to let anyone stray very far from the group."

Coming from George that was an unsettling statement.

"What if one of us chooses to strike out on our own?" Brandon purposely directed the question at Richard.

George without giving Richard time to respond instantly came back with, "As long as it doesn't create a hardship on the rest of us."

Brandon could feel George's words tightening around their necks like a noose. He wondered if leaving the group with food on board Sparrow would somehow fit George's definition of a "hardship". Freedom of choice was slowly withering away with every statement George seemed to make.

Returning to their boats, the lines used to raft the boats together were freed. They slowly started to drift apart as sails were hoisted. George was last to get underway way. He comically made over exaggerated motions to his "green" crewman getting more frustrated by the minute. It made Brandon smile to think the group wasn't distancing themselves from the craziness on shore, at this moment the craziness was bringing up the rear.

The breeze was out of the East and starting to freshen.

"Looks like we're off to a great start," Brandon commented as Sparrow sprung to life coursing through the small swells. Judy altered course slightly to port in order to maintain a comfortable distance from Mark. Richard led the pack with eased sails to equalize his boats superior speed with the slower boats.

"Holding steady at five knots" Judy said, as the group settled into a diamond like formation.

As future weather broadcasts no longer existed the sailors had to rely on cloud identification and barometric pressure to gather weather information. As it was late October the odds of running into a hurricane were low. Hurricanes aside, they still had to keep an eye out for thunderstorms which were practically a daily event. It wasn't the lightning they feared, it was the sudden forty plus mile an hour wind avalanche spilling out ahead of the front that played havoc with their sails. Best case wild ride, worst case getting de-masted. Everyone except the newbies were aware of the hazards.

As evening fell, the moon gave off just enough light to keep track of the fleet. Radio chatter was nonexistent. If it was important they would report it, otherwise it was chalked up as routine. Judy and Brandon prepared for the evenings "two hours on, two hours off" routine for standing watch. Tonight would involve the additional burden of keeping the other boats in sight, avoiding collisions and scanning for intruders. When your watch was over you knew you wouldn't have trouble falling asleep.

Judy volunteered for first watch as Brandon snuggled into his bunk "Wake me up if anything develops". Judy nodded in agreement as he closed his eyes.

It's amazing how fast 2 hours pass when you're tired Brandon thought as Judy woke him to "Your turn."

"Anything happen while I was asleep?"

"I lost track of George for a while."

"It's too bad he showed up, I'd prefer he got lost from the group."

Brandon took the helm as the rest of the first night proved uneventful.

Chapter 7

Current Events

Shortly after sunrise the radio broke the silence. "Everyone listen up, this is Mark, two boats at eleven o'clock. I think there moving away. Looks like one sail, the other power."

George was first to respond, "I don't see anything. Let me know if they look like their heading this way. If they're looking for trouble they've found it, and by the way next time use your number not your name."

"I just got excited."

"Think before you talk next time. 3 out."

That was the first positive sign since leaving port to give the group reason to re-evaluate George's contribution to the fleet. His attitude over the radio not only sent a message of willingness to protect the group but also contained a certain air of bravado.

Mark continued to scan the direction of the potential intruders until they disappeared over the horizon. Mark's discovery of the boats reinforced Brandon and Judy's diligence on keeping a constant 360-degree lookout. If intruders were going to surprise the group, it wasn't going to be due to their negligence.

A number of dolphins joined the fleet as they made their way down the coast. They never failed to draw attention as they effortlessly swam just inside the bow wake of a boat. As their familiar antics were well underway the mood suddenly changed gears. The unmistakable sound of automatic gunfire came from George's boat. You could hear his crew whooping and hollering as volley after volley of bullets pelted the water's surface. The dolphins instantly disappeared back into the sea. Though separated by some distance Brandon and Judy could barely make out, "You got one. No. You got two." from George's crew.

Richard, not wanting to believe what he had just witnessed, broadcast over channel 16.

"Your crew wasn't shooting at the dolphins were they?"

"So what if they were?"

"They say its bad luck to kill a dolphin."

"I don't believe in old wives' tales. Besides, my guys need the target practice."

"And what did they get out of shooting at a stationary target four feet off your bow?"

"Can it #1. Stay off the radio unless it's important."

Richard's inquiry had unintentionally revealed George's attitude toward traditional beliefs and values. The dolphin incident would not be brought up again.

The mild breeze gave way to a stronger wind as the morning progressed. The group managed to roughly stay in formation as their bows turned the oncoming swells into glistening white arrays of spray. Under different circumstances the sailing conditions would have been the epitome of why sailors are drawn to the sea. It's almost impossible to explain to a non-sailor the exhilaration you experience ripping along at six to seven knots by manipulating the awesome power of Mother Nature.

Just before eleven o'clock Richard reported another sighting. "Listen up, large ship heading straight for us. What do you guys want to do?"

After what seemed like a long silence Richard came back over the radio, "Look, we can't out run it so we have two choices, stay in place or scatter in different directions."

The choice of running away would not favor Sparrow, she was the smallest boat of the group, and lacking a diesel engine would be the easiest to capture.

George was the first to submit an alternative, "Why don't we try to hail it on channel 16? What do we have to loose. I don't think a ship is going to waste their time messing around with a few tiny boats."

He was right. Their threats would come in the form of smaller boats looking for resources to extend a not so certain future.

"This is 2, I agree."

"4, affirmative."

"Works for us, go for it, 3 out."

As Richard started transmitting on channel 16 the ship slightly altered course to its port side. To everyone's relief the white ship revealed the unmistakable red stripe of the United States Coast Guard. The ship did not display any intention of slowing down.

"This is the Coast Guard, over."

"Is there anything you can tell us about what's going on? Over."

"We were informed a nationwide power outage exists. Over."

"Is there any place along the coast that's safe for us to anchor at? Over."

"Negative. Over."

"Any advice or recommendations for us? Over."

"Avoid the coastline until order is restored. Over and out."

The ship continually shrank against the horizon as quickly as it had appeared. They were obviously heading north at top speed for reasons unknown.

Thanks to the chance encounter with the Coast Guard ship, the rumors that preceded their escape would finally have substance. This was real, and from a credible source worse, than they had feared. Any reliance on outside aid was obviously nonexistent. Their survival would totally depend on making as few mistakes as possible until order was restored.

"Well guys, it looks like we're definitely on our own from here on out."

Richard continued to lead the group in the direction of the Dry Tortuga's as the afternoon wore on.

Judy caught a glimpse of Jordan cleaning a rifle aboard George's boat. The barrel periodically reflecting a flash from the late afternoon sun. "Looks like their preparing for a war over there."

"Yeah, let's hope it doesn't come down to that or we're toast."

One thing Brandon regretted was selling his shotgun in California. Originally planning to cruise the Bahamas and Mexico, Judy had read articles about people having their boats seized for carrying weapons. He knew it would be risky hiding his Smith & Wesson .45 on board, but the benefit of being able to protect themselves outweighed the risk of losing the boat. Besides, there was no easy way to hide a shotgun. If they hadn't kept his gun the closest thing to a weapon would have been their flare gun.

As the sun settled below the horizon Brandon stood the first watch. Over the last few days he had come to the conclusion an attack at night was highly unlikely. The moon didn't rise to illuminate the night till the wee hours just before dawn. Unless someone was careless enough to display lights you wouldn't see them at all. Brandon thought to himself, maybe that's why the Indians didn't attack at night, they needed time to size up the enemy. Still, scanning an uneventful area of the dark had to be maintained.

Years before, Brandon had earned a pilot's license to get over his fear of flying. One of the tricks he remembered from night flying was not to stare directly at an object in the dark. Any dim source of light would magically disappear. Our brains subconsciously fill in an object with the surrounding black sky. He did his best to use peripheral vision but with his failing eye sight he probably wouldn't have seen the Titanic.

What the scanning lacked, keeping track of the other boats in the group made up for. By the end of the watch your eyes were so tired that nothing was more rewarding than crawling into your bunk for a couple of hours sleep.

Chapter 8

Dry Tortuga's

The morning sun found them within a couple of hours of a well anticipated anchorage at the Dry Tortuga's.

As they closed on the island destination, Judy started reading about the Dry Tortuga's from their "Cruising the Bahamas" guide. She relayed a condensed version to Brandon.

"The Dry Tortuga's were first discovered in 1513. The word "Dry" was added to indicate a lack of water. The United States built a fort on the island. It was also used as a prison after the Civil War. In 1742 the crew of the HMS Tyger wrecked just offshore of the island. The stranded crew lived on the island for fifty-six days before sailing to Jamaica in several small boats. Do you want me to continue reading?"

Brandon shook his head no. Something dead ahead had caught his attention. He slowly raised his right hand to shield his eyes from the morning sun, turned to Judy and announced "Land Ho".

He knew it was a corny thing to say but couldn't resist. Judy would chalk it up to him watching too many old time sailing movies.

"Look straight ahead, we're about 20 minutes away."

As the boats approached from the leeward, or downwind side of the island the large outline of the fort began to take form. The fort looked surreal perched on such a small island surrounded by white sand and blue water.

Maneuvering around the island it soon became apparent they were not going to have the island to themselves. A dozen or more fairly large power boats lay anchored about 150 feet offshore. Curiously, no visible signs of life could be detected on any of the boats. If they were under surveillance the occupants did a good job of keeping themselves concealed.

As they approached the island they maintained a safe distance from the powerboat anchorage. The crystal clear water helped aid in their decision of where to drop anchor. They carefully avoided anchoring near the beautiful yet dangerous coral reefs randomly growing just below the water's surface.

Whether it be a mistake or not the decision to go ashore was made. The calculated risk was based on the fact that they had gotten this close to the island without incidence. As a positive gesture they would fly a small white flag on Mark's dinghy to display their peaceful intentions.

Brandon, Mark and George volunteered to go ashore. They instinctively arranged their seating positions to balance the dinghy for the short ride to the shore. The trip to the island would take about four minutes. As they closed to within 75 feet of the shoreline, half a dozen men wearing military fatigues and armed with semi-automatic rifles exited the fort. Moving in an orderly fashion they lined up to intersect the dinghy on the beach.

Brandon in a hushed voice uttered "This doesn't look good", as he and Mark decided to let George do the talking. George concealed his pistol as to not escalate tensions.

As the dinghy gently beached on the white sand the leader of the group raised his hand making the universal "Halt" gesture. "Hold it right there. State your intentions."

Their guns were held in a ready position. None of the guns directly aimed at the dinghy's occupants. The landing party suddenly realize they were unwelcome intruders on this recently acquired turf.

"We're just passing through on our way south." replied George.

Brandon, Mark and George kept their hands motionless, as well as in plain sight. This was not a group you wanted to spook by unnecessary hand movement.

"And your reason for stopping here?"

"We've been sailing awhile and were hoping to get off the boats and stretch our legs a bit."

The leader carefully masked any emotions as he spoke, "That's not going to happen on this island."

Recognizing the benefits of possibly joining this group, George bluntly asked, "You wouldn't be in need of another person who can handle a gun?"

"No. We're not taking in strangers. You need to go back to your boats."

Judging by their paramilitary manner, this group had carefully prepared to take full possession of the island at the first sign of a country in crisis. As Brandon looked beyond the men he noticed more armed soldiers strategically placed along breaks in the wall that once housed cannons. This definitely was a well-organized and equipped small army. You could only pity anyone who was careless enough to try and crash their party.

"We'd appreciate it if we could stay anchored where we are for a short spell."

The leader turned to face the other men in his command. After conferring with what appeared to be the second in command, he turned back and stated in no uncertain terms, "We'll let you stay twenty-four hours. Do not try to sneak ashore. If you are caught on the island you will be shot on sight without warning."

Though the meeting could have gone better, it was apparent they were not the least bit interested in removing what life supporting provisions the little boats carried. At least not at this time. How long could they survive on the small island without acquiring outside food and fuel was anybody's guess, but for now, it appeared safe.

"No problem, thanks for giving us a day. We'll be out of here tomorrow morning."

As they motored their way back to the boats the island "Welcoming Committee" returned to the fort. Sentries located along the wall kept close watch as the dinghy departed.

Motoring back Mark brought up the obvious, "Those guys are brilliant. Take a well-armed group of men and take possession of an abandoned fort 70 miles offshore on an island. A fucking fort on an island! Absolutely Brilliant! They don't even have to worry about hurricanes, that fort's been there for at least a hundred years and still standing."

Brandon had once read there were probably a thousand or more private paramilitary type compounds in the United States, the majority tucked away in hilly or mountainous terrain. It never crossed his mind one would be located on an island, let alone one offering the protection of a former fort.

"I think we should definitely avoid this place on the way back."

George and Mark shook their heads in agreement.

Mark adding, "If we ever come back."

Re-uniting on Richard's boat they retold in detail what had just transpired. The opportunity to scavenge the island for resources was soundly denied. The only comfort afforded by the island came in the form of a brief respite from sailing and a short window to relax in. As if that were truly possible under the circumstances.

As strange as it felt, a calm did fall over Brandon realizing not every outsider or group was evil or out to plunder. The fort represented a form of order and protection for the small population within its walls. If it existed here, there was hope. The only challenge was finding it elsewhere, a society willing to take in refugees.

As Brandon reflected on the day's events he felt uneasy thinking how easy it was for George to volunteer to abandon the group at the first perceived opportunity. Could he be relied upon if things got tough? Probably not. Would he stay with the fleet if he felt they had nothing to offer? Again probably not. The real question was what was important enough for him to want to tag along with the group. The obvious answer was food. Brandon knew sooner or later they would have to deal with George and his crew. It would give a whole new meaning to the phrase "food fight".

The monotony of standing watch that night was broken by the sound of music and laughter emanating from within the fort. The boats were anchored downwind of the island. The distinct aroma of bar-b-cued meat intermingled in the mild offshore breeze. Brandon found it hard to scan a dark ocean that night. His thoughts eventually drifted in and out of happier moments in his life.

Shortly after midnight Brandon's sleep was interrupted by Judy lightly shaking his shoulder.

"Brandon get up."

He groggily replied "Don't tell me it's my watch already?"

"No, but it's starting to rain. Let's rig the water catch."

Their water catch amounted to a triangular piece of waterproof material with a hose type fitting in the middle. The catch was attached by short lengths of rope at the corners allowing it to form an upside down belly, funneling water to the center. The device was a simplistic way to harvest life sustaining liquid. The couple knew they could only survive about 3 days without water. In this warm climate, maybe less. As conservative as they were, Brandon and Judy had depleted about a quarter of their water supply. The unexpected rain afforded them the opportunity to top off their tank.

With the morning light, the small fleet prepped their boats for departure. The island appeared as uninhabited as Brandon's first sighting. Sails were raised and as they slowly sailed away Brandon knew there would be no farewell party from the islanders wishing them good luck. From the reception they encountered on the beach it would more likely have been good riddance!

Chapter 9

Wicked

The previous night's rain proved to be the vanguard for wicked weather ahead. Wind and waves continued to build in intensity as the barometer steadily fell. Not knowing if this was just a passing tropical storm, or worse, the forefront of a hurricane, the intrepid sailors configured their boats for battle against Mother Nature.

The sea had transformed yesterday's sparkling blue water into shades of green and white as the wind continued to whip the water into a relentless legion of steep cascading waves. This was sailing at its worst. There would be no "time out" until the storm subsided.

At first sign of deteriorating conditions, Judy and Brandon followed time tested procedures as they readied Sparrow for the upcoming fight for survival. Jack lines were secured fore and aft. The rugged jack line straps minimized the danger of detachment from Sparrow. The last thing you wanted to see was your boat sailing away without you. One end of a short strap or tether attached directly to the jack line. The other end attached to a ring on Brandon and Judy's life jackets. In the event they fell overboard the tether would keep them securely attached alongside Sparrow until they could be safely pulled back onboard.

Having rigged the jack lines, they now turned their attention to reducing sail. If there was one golden rule on Sparrow, it was drop the mainsail in strong winds. Sparrow, being a cutter rig ketch, could easily maintain hull speed with just the two small head sails and rear mizzen. Dropping the mainsail also gave the added benefit of considerably reducing the amount of heel or tilt. Speed at this point was not a consideration. Keeping just enough water moving past the rudder to maintain steerage was. The rest amounted to just holding on for the ride.

The wind driven saltwater started to sting Brandon's eyes. He had to shout to get Judy's attention over the howling wind. "I've lost track of everyone, do you see them?"

"You're kidding; I can't see anything."

In addition to violently rolling side to side, Sparrow was now beginning to hobby horse fore and aft as she crawled up the incoming waves and slid down their backsides.

Judy now had to shout over the fury of the storm, "This is the roughest weather I've ever sailed in!"

Brandon didn't say anything. He continued tending to the foresails as Judy did her best to keep the boat on course. Keeping on course now defined as "Path of least resistance". They did everything they could think of to lessen the strain on Sparrow's rigging as she violently forged forward.

At a certain point fatigue starts to set in. The constant strain of maintaining your balance takes its toll. Stiff muscles coupled with relentless motion eventually brings you to the point of wanting to scream "enough", but you know you'd be shouting at deaf ears. Your only comfort was knowing it would eventually come to an end.

Brandon decided it was time to relieve Judy from the stress of helming the boat. She had been fighting the wind and water for the last 2 hours.

"Let's trade."

"Are you sure, I can steer a little longer."

Brandon had to smile as he thought back on Judy earning the nickname "Helm Hog". She could steer a boat for hours on end and always seemed reluctant to share the duty. He knew under these conditions she had to be tired and admired her resilience. Knowing her, she probably felt more concerned with his welfare than her own.

"I'm positive, let's trade!"

Normally, relieving her on the helm would have been an easy task. Trading places in this storm now required careful timing and balance. Never was the saying, "One hand for the ship, and one hand for yourself" more applicable.

Having successfully switched positions, Judy placed her back against the cabin trunk which offered little protection from the wind driven rain. She held on to the jib sheet ready to release tension should Sparrow violently start to broach. On a small boat with a two-person crew there is no go down into the cabin and rest, you only traded one miserable job for another miserable job.

The storm lasted approximately seven hours. Sparrow sailed out of the melee in one piece. Judy was finally able to enter the cabin and whip together something for them to eat. She reappeared ten minutes later bearing chicken noodle soup and a much appreciated cup of hot coffee.

The wind and the rain may have passed but the steep waves left behind would continue to toss Sparrow around for the next couple of hours. Judy insisted on taking first watch, and after a few minutes of back and forth discussion, Brandon conceded and went below for a couple of hours' rest. As far as Brandon and Judy were concerned what they had just endured was as close to their definition of a "Perfect Storm" as they ever wanted to know.

The gulf slowly settled into her typical picture postcard looking image. The waves were still larger than normal, but beautiful just the same. From their original position and heading before the storm hit they carefully plotted a course that would hopefully reunite them with the fleet.

Twelve hours later the tranquil setting gave way to excitement as Judy announced, "We've got company!", as she pointed in the direction of a sailboat some distance from their position. "Think it's one of ours?"

Brandon exited the cabin with what he calls his U-Boat Commander binoculars. "I can't tell from here, but it could be George. Yeah, it looks like a 32 footer."

Judy took a turn but like Brandon couldn't make a positive identification. "It doesn't seem to be moving. Maybe they're going slow to give us a chance to catch up."

That sounded reasonable to Brandon as he slightly altered course for the drifting boat. As they closed the distance it soon became apparent it was not one of their party.

"Check it out. The mast is bent pretty badly. No wonder it's not moving. The storm must have played hell with it."

Judy carefully inspected the boat from the safety of the binoculars. Slowly passing the transom she informed Brandon, "The name of the boat is "Sanity". It's says Key West under the name."

Brandon couldn't help but comment, "Great name for a boat in an insane world."

"I don't think we should get to close to it. I don't see anybody moving around." Thirty feet from the lifeless vessel Judy cupped her hands around her mouth as she shouted, "Hello, anyone on board....hello....hello." Her hail was met with silence. Not a good sign. It looked like the storm had claimed one or more victims.

Brandon slowly circled the boat thinking out loud, "Looks bad, bent mast, torn sails. Beat up yes, but unless they went overboard definitely survivable."

As they neared completion of the circle Judy in a puzzled tone asked, "What happened to the hull? It looks like chunks of fiberglass are missing on this side."

As the now derelict boat no longer appeared to pose a threat Brandon suggested they tie-up alongside and try to piece together what had taken place. Judy asked Brandon if he wanted her to get his gun.

"You gotta be kidding. If I thought there was going to be trouble I wouldn't be going aboard."

Brandon cautiously climbed onto the disabled boat. After slowly scanning the topsides he entered the cabin. Minutes passed as Judy anxiously awaited Brandon's findings. Unlike his cautious entry he suddenly bolted out of the cabin and back onto Sparrow.

"Untie the boat. Let's get out of here."

Judy sensed Brandon's findings weren't storm related.

"What happened?"

"The people aren't missing because of the storm. They were shot."

"You saw their bodies?"

"No, but with all the blood splattered inside the cabin what would you think. Those chunks in the hull were made by bullets. The boat has been completely ransacked. They probably looked like sitting ducks with a bent mast. Easy pickings for scavengers."

Judy remained silent as Brandon continued. "The sooner we find the group the better. This is looking real scary. We're getting to close to land. What are we, 25 miles from Key West?"

"If that. The keys have a big boating population. We're lucky we haven't seen more boats."

They quickly resumed pursuit of their now illusive companions. They realized they were totally on their own. The prospect of making contact with any of the fleet after the storm was next to none.

Judy and Brandon had just witnessed with their own eyes the severe penalty a single boat could face on the high seas. They knew the only difference between Sparrow suffering Sanity's fate, was Sanity being in the wrong place at the right time.

Chapter 10

Choice Point

Sparrow now faced the most daunting leg of the trip. The final destination, Bight of Acklins Island lay about 494 nautical miles south east of their present location. The route they were taking was sure to be traveled by an armada of boats fleeing the United States.

Dark blue water now paved their way forward. Dolphins swimming alongside Sparrow gave a false sense of peace and harmony by masking the brutal reality that loomed just beyond the visible horizon.

The once pleasurable act of crossing paths with another adventure bound boat now induced fear and anxiety. There would be no exchanging of waves or hailing each other over the radio. Survival now depended on creating as much distance from other boats as possible.

As anxiety waned, Brandon and Judy settled into the more mundane chores aboard the boat. Studying the chart plotter, Brandon estimated it would take at least five days to reach the island. Judy had spent the last thirty minutes reviewing the state of their food and water supplies. Satisfied with her findings she reported, "We're doing excellent. Twenty-three gallons of water left and we've hardly put a dent in the food. What do you want for dinner?"

Brandon was not a picky eater, "Make it easy on yourself. Fix whatever you're in the mood for."

As Judy went below Brandon knew she would have no problem coming up with a delicious meal. Brandon on the other hand only dealt with cooking on the most elemental level. Judy found cooking the meals rewarding, especially when the alternative was letting Brandon loose in the galley.

The late afternoon sun slowly revealed the unmistakable form of a sailboat some distance off. They had spotted three boats earlier that morning but unlike the previous encounters, this one didn't vanish into obscurity. Brandon took evasive action pulling the tiller toward his hip as Sparrow tacked hard over. The abrupt change in direction now sent Brandon tracking away from his intended course. He planned on returning to the original heading as soon as the shadowing boat lost interest. The game of cat and mouse was full on.

The pursuing boat was much larger and faster than Sparrow. After an hour of zigzagging it became apparent they couldn't out run the persistent yacht. Brandon had ignored multiple hails from the larger boat on the radio during the chase, but now as the boat closed to within two hundred feet found it in his best interest to make contact. If for no other reason than being forewarned of the pursuer's intentions. Radio silence would have to be broken.

"Sparrow hailing large sailboat off my stern. Over."

"Sparrow, this is Wanderlust. Where are you headed? Over"

It was obvious they were interested in Sparrow's original heading prior to Brandon's ill-fated attempt at evasion. He knew disclosure of their true destination could have an adverse effect on the group. One George was enough. It was impossible to know if the Wanderlust carried enough food to support themselves over the course of several months.

"Nowhere in particular. We're just trying to avoid the mainland...Over."

"Yeah, that's are plan too. What's your home port? We're from Miami."

Brandon felt more comfortable sensing the Wanderlust bore them no immediate harm. If Brandon and Judy had truly struck out on their own the larger boat would have been viewed as a welcome companion.

"Saint Petersburg area."

"Wow, long way. You didn't have any trouble getting this far south?"

"Besides the storm, we came across a couple of boats. One was set on fire, the other brutally attacked."

"Any survivors?"

"None that we could see."

"Sounds like what we left behind in Miami."

A few seconds later the stranger's voice came back over the radio.

"Well Sparrow, you're welcome to keep us company if you'd like. Think it over and let us know."

Brandon and Judy spent the next hour agonizing over the pros and cons of Wanderlust's gracious offer. There was no guarantee the rest of their group would meet up at the island. But, selling out for pleasant safe company bobbing around in an unsafe Atlantic would only last for so long. Besides, how would they fair if suddenly attacked. Images of the "Sanity" tipped the scale. At least with the group they could probably count on George going out in a blaze of glory defending the pact.

The decision to reject Wanderlust's offer was made. The couple carefully scripted a reply that would cordially thank the proposal, but ultimately decline the offer without jeopardizing their real agenda.

"Wanderlust, we want to thank you for the offer. Sparrow is in relatively good shape. You can cover a lot of ground faster without us tagging along. There's probably a lot of destitute families floating around that could really use your support."

"Are you sure you can make it out here on your own?"

"We're positive."

"Well, take care and keep your eyes open."

Parting ways Brandon once again resumed his original course as the Wanderlust slowly disappeared over the horizon.

As darkness fell upon a moonless night they once again enjoyed the freedom of the dark. The odds of being detected would be practically nonexistent over the next eleven hours. Occasionally they would notice dim lit objects at great distances, probably freighters or cruise ships stranded and confused as to where to go next. The rest of the evening was only interrupted by watch changes.

The morning seascape reflected the drab gray colors of an approaching late summer squall. Unlike the storm they had just experienced a squall packed all bad parts into a fifteen-minute show. Deadly lightning, torrential downpours and fifty-mile an hour winds where a given. There was no dodging this giant.

Scrambling to secure everything below deck, they then braced themselves in the cockpit. Luckily this short battle was going to take place in daylight. As the front steadily approached, the light steady breeze suddenly gave way to an avalanche of strong wind. Sparrow violently heeled over putting her leeward rail into the now dark gray sea. The roar of the howling wind gave voice to the pandemonium, only overshadowed by the unnerving sound of echoing thunder.

Squalls were practically a daily event during the summer in Palmetto. Sparrow safely tied in her slip had nothing to fear. Brandon and Judy actually enjoyed the wild display that never lasted more than five to ten minutes. The passing of a squall gave the rain soaked marina the luxury of transforming a hot humid late afternoon temperature into a cool evening breeze. But, they weren't safely tied in the slip. Now they were faced with two choices, drop sail and use the motor to steer into the wind or, use a tactic known as heaving-to. The maneuver required completing a tack, but not allowing the jib sails to reposition on the opposite side of the bow. If properly executed the "heaving-to" maneuver would stall Sparrow's forward movement while at the same time allowing her to maintain a reasonable bow into the wind stance.

The tactic worked and Sparrow rode out the wild weather no worse for wear. As the wind gradually returned to a more benign state, the last remnant of the squall came in the form of diminishing rain.

Chapter 11

Paradise?

Brandon and Judy had left Florida well prepared for survival in a world that no longer provided basic human needs. Soon the farms and dairies that once fed a hungry nation would vanish. The trucks that practically delivered food to your door would no longer travel the nation's freeways. Canned and manufactured foods would rapidly be a thing of the past. The only nourishment available would be what you possessed, and you damn well wouldn't trade it for a few worthless pieces of gold or silver. Barter, which worked in the age of abundance would soon take on the form of acquisition by brute force.

Refugees seeking safety from the land of the lost would not be welcomed with open arms. Countries that once catered to American tourist dollars would shortly suffer the same fate. How they would be received by the sparse population on the tiny islands remained to be seen. There were just too many unknowns this early in the game.

During the twilight hours just before dawn, the unmistakable shape a small island matched the GPS coordinates they had been given. The small island heralded the completion of their escape.

Richard and Mark's decision to relocate to a small island in the Exuma's out island chain was perfect. The sparsely populated smaller islands would make their presence indistinguishable from the hundreds of boats who visited the islands annually on vacation. Many of the larger islands hosted plantations dating to the Revolutionary War. If there was a "fly in the ointment" it was a lack of freshwater. Luckily for the group, each boat carried a water maker of one form or another capable of rendering freshwater from the sea.

The island they chose contained numerous outcroppings of trees, mangroves and other bush type plants. The snow-white powdery sand along the beach stood in sharp contrast against the aqua marine warm Bahamian water. The trees, a mix of palm and other varieties local to the area, would furnish relief from the blazing sun as well as mask their homesteading activities from the locals. The islands were remote enough that word of America's plight would probably take weeks to spread from island to island.

The final task amounted to locating the rest of the group. The anticipation of getting off Sparrow and standing on solid ground would be a welcome relief.

As they sailed into the small cove, Judy couldn't help but comment, "Wow, the island is beautiful. If you have to sit out the end of the world this place has my vote."

Brandon shook his head in agreement.

Radio silence no longer mattered this far from home. Brandon picked up the VHF mic and announced over the radio, "This is Sparrow. Anyone copy?"

Brandon repeated the call three times before receiving a reply.

"Sparrow, glad to see you made it."

The voice was unmistakably George's.

"Anyone else make it?"

"Yeah, they're all here. I can see you from where I am. Look to your ten o'clock."

Judy quickly checked out the area to her left with binoculars. "I can just see the tops of the masts behind that clump of trees." She pointed the position out.

"Great George, Judy sees the boats. We'll see you in a few minutes."

George radioed back "Bring your gun with you."

"Why, are we expecting trouble?"

"No, but we need to be prepared."

Sparrow quietly motored over to where the other boats were anchored. They found a spot that would keep Sparrow a safe distance from the other boats while allowing plenty of room to swing with the changing wind and tides. Judy monitoring the depth sounder readings from the cockpit let Brandon know when to drop the anchor. They felt comfortable anchoring in ten feet of water. Brandon let out seventy feet of the anchor rode as Judy put the motor into reverse. The maneuver allowed the anchor to securely set itself deep into the sandy bottom.

The last order of business was tying off loose items on deck and putting on Sparrow's sail covers on. Judy pulled the dinghy alongside Sparrow's port side. With Sparrow's low freeboard stepping into the dinghy was an easy transition. A few pulls on the starter rope and the small outboard engine powered the dinghy forward for the short trip to the shore.

As they approached the beach Brandon happened to notice Jordan sitting in the shade of a palm tree with his rifle pointing in their direction. What happened next would completely sour the reunion. The T-shirt Jordan was wearing bore the name "Sanity" in bold letters across his chest.

"Judy, look at the T-shirt Jordan's wearing!"

"Seems like your instincts were right all along. Let's just keep it under wraps until we can talk to the rest of the guys privately."

Though Brandon never saw the dead bodies of the people on board, fate had managed to point a finger at George and his crew as the deadly assassins involved in the brutal slaughter of Sanity's crew. Visions of the blood splattered interior of the boat were deeply embedded in Brandon's mind.

Upon reaching the beach they drug the small dinghy far enough away from the light surf to prevent it from slipping back into the sea at high tide. They walked toward George standing near the tree line. Brandon started to piece together why the others in the group weren't there to greet them on their arrival.

"Welcome to my little island. I think this place is going to work out. I've found an old house we're turning into a sort of defensible compound."

"I'll have Mike show you where we're hiding the dinghies a little later but for now just leave yours here. You'll need it to bring supplies back a little later on. Jordan's keeping an eye on the boats."

"Why was Jordan pointing his rifle at us?"

"I'll explain everything to you when we reach house."

Brandon and Judy wished they would have arrived a little sooner. Brandon found the "My little island" an odd choice of words.

"Follow me, it's a short way up the trail."

"How'd you find it?"

"The boys and I did a little scouting as soon as we hit the beach."

"And the house was empty?"

"Not at first. We sort of persuaded the old codgers that were living there to leave."

"How'd you do that?"

George tapped the side of his rifle and smiled. "They might have been old, but they weren't stupid."

Was this a part of their new reality? Had they transformed into the kind of people they were fleeing from? Were they somehow unwilling co-participants in the brutalizing of boaters and terrorizing the locals? Brandon and Judy didn't say a word as they trailed behind George. Their thoughts were bursting with questions to ask when they reached the house or as George called it "compound."

As the trail made a final bend, a small deteriorated house came into view. Years of neglect had taken its toll. Even in its glory days it wouldn't have had much to offer beyond basic shelter from the elements. A short distance from the house sat a shed probably used at one time to house the small tractor now rusting away near the back of the house.

"Well, this is it. Everyone has to pull their own weight around here. Hang tight a few minutes while I figure out a schedule for the two of you. I wasn't sure you would make it with the storm and all. By the way I'll need you to give me your gun."

"What for?"

"Because I'm in charge now."

"And what if I don't?"

"Take a look at Mike."

Brandon slowly turned to look in Mike's direction and was startled to see his rifle pointing at them.

"I see I don't have any choice in the matter."

"You always have a choice."

Brandon handed him the gun.

George turned and entered the house. The front door and walls of the house stripped of paint bore witness to the ravages of untold storms and hurricanes over the years. A deep sway had formed in the rotting rafters of the roof. The sagging roofline was reminiscent of old barns as they seemed to slowly implode by decay back into the soil of their creation.

Mark and LuAnn sat resting in the shade some distance off. They half-heartedly gave a wave to Brandon and Judy as they awaited George's return.

Mike sat on the porch, rifle in hand, keeping close watch over the site. Brandon thought it curious he would choose that spot to protect the compound. He seemed more interested in the activities of the group than keeping watch for strangers.

The familiar sound of Richard's voice speaking to Amanda broke the silence as they entered the camp. Richard was pushing a rusty old wheelbarrow filled with dried tree branches. They hadn't noticed Brandon and Judy standing near the front porch as they approached.

"Richard, glad to see you made it. Why did George take away my gun?"

"That's the first thing he made us do when we got on the island."

Richard sat the wheelbarrow down on its legs. He walked over and gave Judy a hug as he simultaneously extended his arm to shake hands with Brandon.

Brandon asked Richard, "When did you get here?"

"We got here yesterday. Unfortunately, George beat us to the island."

"Judy and I have a few interesting things to tell you about the trip."

Mike suddenly developed an interest in their conversation as he turned to hear them better.

"You might want to wait until you've settled in. I have a few things to tell you as well."

Brandon realized Richard did not want to discuss what was going on in front of Mike.

George exited the front door. "There will be plenty of time for chit chat later. Right now I need everyone working. Chop, chop, Richard."

George's tone clearly sent a message. It wasn't a request. It was an order. George approached them carrying a small notebook.

"This is what I want you guys to do. Judy's going to help LuAnn cook, wash clothes and whatever else women are good at. You're going to use your dinghy to ferry supplies from the boats."

Brandon felt uneasy about boarding and unloading Mark and Richard's boats.

"Why do we have to live on the island? Why not just stay on our boats?"

"It's too hard to protect all of you on the water. My job is to keep our supplies out of the wrong hands."

"And the others thought that was cool?"

George smiled but didn't answer the question. "As to the sleeping arrangements Mike, Jordan and I sleep in the house. You guys sleep in the tractor shack."

"Sleep on what?"

"I had Mark and Richard bring over their quarter berth cushions yesterday. The first thing you will do today is get yours and bring them to the shed. If they are good enough for the boats they are good enough for the shed."

"What about taking a crap?"

Brandon's relentless stream of questions were starting to irritate George.

"That's enough questions. I'm sure you guys will figure something out. Right now I want you to start bringing back the food on Mark's boat."

"Where do I put the food when I come back?"

"The house. It's my job to protect the food."

Brandon thought how convenient for George, Mike and Jordan. "Do I get any help?"

"No, the others have their own work assignments. Like I said everyone pulls their own weight around here. Make sure you bring back a couple of blankets and some warm clothes. It gets kind of cold in the shed at night."

Chapter 12

Living Hell

Brandon spent the rest of the afternoon using the dinghy to ferry supplies back to camp. LuAnn, like Judy, had managed to stash food in every available nook and cranny she could find. The dinghy only held a small shopping carts worth of food forcing Brandon to make half a dozen round trips from Mark's boat to the house. It was tiring work. The relentless squeak, squeak, squeak of the wheelbarrows dry axle only served to heighten the tension. As he rolled the last load of food to the back door of the house Judy informed him they would be eating soon.

During the day Brandon had noticed Richard transforming an interior door from the house into a picnic type table. The table sat surrounded by two bench seats on each side fashioned from planks sitting on top of rusty five gallon buckets. It was obvious eating from now on would be an outside affair.

The women did their best to hide the crudeness of the "dining room table" by utilizing a blue tarp from one of the boats as a tablecloth cover. Dishes adorned with nautical flags, knives, forks and glasses also recently transferred to the island, created a festive look. The scene resembled a family picnic in a park.

Amanda exited the rear door banging a large pot with a ladle.

"Dinner time. Dinner everyone!"

Brandon was looking forward to finally having the opportunity to sit down and talk to Richard and Mark.

The men gathered at one end of the table as Judy brought out a large pot half full of stew. Any illusions of a family picnic went out the door as Judy served two small scoops of stew on each plate. LuAnn followed Judy filling their glasses with water.

Brandon lost control.

"That's all we get? I worked my ass off all day and that's it! Two small scoops of stew? You got to be kidding!"

Judy spoke for the kitchen crew.

"That's all we're entitled to eat according to George. He made me leave half the pot for them in the kitchen. He thinks guard duty entitles them to more food."

"That brings up my first question. Who put George in charge?"

"George put George in charge" Richard, mumbled in a low voice."

"Why didn't you just…"

Brandon was cut off by Judy making a "shush" sound as George, Mike and Jordan walked out of the house and made their way toward the table.

"I want you guys to step it up. If you wanna eat your gonna have to work harder or starve. I don't want to see anyone dragging ass tomorrow."

Jordan and Mike with rifles in hand smiled as they took up position behind Brandon and Richard.

"Really George? These guys look pretty beat to me. What's so important we have to bust ass?"

Brandon could see the other members at the table instantly tense up. Mike standing behind Brandon took a step forward and without warning whacked Brandon's shoulder with the butt of his rifle. The impact of the blow practically knocking him to the ground.

"Number one rule on my island don't ever question my authority. Do I make myself clear?"

Mike started to raise his rifle butt for another blow prompting Brandon to concede, "Yeah, I get it."

"Good. This brings me to rule number two. In order to make sure you follow my orders your "significant other" will be held responsible for your actions. In other words, if you fuck up they're going to pay the price."

Everyone sat in complete silence as George turned and walked back into the house. Mike and Jordan walked over to the front porch and sat down on the small step. They seemed to closely observe the group's reaction to George's new set of rules.

Mark speaking just above a whisper broke the silence.

"What the hell is happening? He's out of his fricking mind!"

Richard quietly added, "He was trouble the minute we stepped foot on the island. I really didn't think he'd go this far. This is the first time he's used force to make a point. Now he's threatening to punish the women?"

Brandon began to realize the pain in his shoulder was a direct result of George probing the group's reaction as he slowly raised control over them to the next level. With Mike and Jordan observing their conversation it became clear any discussion of George would have to wait for the privacy of the shed later that evening.

The women cleared the table as the men discussed events they had encountered on the voyage to the island. All shared one or more similar stories. Brandon chose to remain silent about his encounter with "Sanity" and the t-shirt linking George and his crew to the violence and mayhem. The table conversation carefully danced around any subject that could ignite George's implementation of "rule number two". An hour or so later the sun began to set as they made their way toward the tractor shed.

The group entered the old garage. The musty smell of dirt, oil and old rotting wood permeated the air. A sail from one of the boats had been placed on the ground to protect the quarter berth cushions from the soil. The shed lacked windows for illumination. Rusty hinges were the only trace where a garage door once separated the room from the elements. A smaller sail attached to the opening now served as the door. Much needed ventilation was provided by the open cracks in the 1X6 planks used for the walls.

Everyone pulled their cushion closer forming a circle in the center of the room. Richard had Amanda keep watch on Jordan through one of the large cracks in the wall. With no light source in the garage it was easy to conceal their movements from the guards. Earlier George had ordered Mike to get some sleep and relieve Jordan around midnight.

Brandon was first to speak. "We need to come up with a plan. Any ideas?"

"Whatever we come up with it's got to work the first time." Richard replied, "I don't want anything happening to Amanda."

"Do you really think if push came to shove they'd kill us?" Mark asked.

"I don't think; I know they would. Judy and I came across a 32-foot sailboat right after the big storm. The only trace of the crew was blood splatter and bullet holes."

"What makes you think George had anything to do with that boat?"

"The name of the boat was "Sanity."

Richard spoke up, "Sanity, I've seen that name before."

"Yeah Richard, yesterday Jordan was wearing a T-shirt with the name "Sanity" across the chest."

Brandon had just given the group invaluable insight as to the depths George, Mike and Jordan were capable of going if push came to shove. The next two hours were spent in quiet discussion of escape strategies before calling it a night.

As the sun broke through the morning haze the familiar sound of a banging pot announced breakfast. This time two scoops of oatmeal along with a little sugar filled the small bowls. There was no way in hell you wouldn't be starving by dinner time. Hell, you were still starving after you ate George's anemic breakfast portions.

"Well, check it out" said Mark, as LuAnn came out of the house carrying a pot of coffee in one hand and cups in the other.

"George is going all out on breakfast today."

Mark's wisecrack eased the tension around the table. The relaxed atmosphere of sitting around enjoying a cup of coffee with friends would soon be replaced as George approached the table.

"Yesterday Jordan thought he heard voices some distance off. I want him to take the three of you and make sure we're the only ones on the island."

Mike without thinking replied, "Maybe you shouda asked the old..."

"Shut your mouth!" George scowled as he quickly spun around towards Mike.

As George turned to face the men again, Mike's face turned dark red with anger. It was the same kind of anger Brandon had witnessed over the cigarettes. Mike hated being reprimanded, especially in front of the other men. He appeared to be the type to take his embarrassment out on the next available person in the group be it male or female.

"Like I said, find out what's going on. Work as a team. Jordan will be keeping an eye on you, Mike's going to stay back and keep an eye on the women."

The men filed behind Jordan as they walked past the house. Mike standing just out of George's view, smiled as he held his fists shoulder high grinding his hips in and out simulating the motion of having sex. Brandon knew his antics were meant to regain his power and control over the group by inciting rage and torment among the men. Anyone foolish enough to be baited into losing their temper would subject Judy, LuAnn or Amanda to the whim and will of their sadistic captors. Instead of finding a place of safe refuge on the tiny island Brandon and Judy had found themselves the latest inhabitants of

"Living Hell, Population 9."

Chapter 13

Cupid Strikes

As the men dispersed into the tree line George ordered Judy and Amanda to take the five-gallon plastic jerry cans over to Mark's boat. Filling the containers and returning to camp would take a couple of hours. In addition to the water, George had noticed quite a few bottles of wine and liquor on Richard's boat the night of the meeting in the marina. He wanted them brought back as well. LuAnn, whom he seemed to have an attraction toward, was ordered to remain on the grounds for laundry duty. Mike sat at the front porch cleaning his rifle.

Judy and Amanda rolled the squeaky wheelbarrow full of empty plastic water cans down the path toward the dinghies. They worried about LuAnn being left alone in the camp.

"Think she'll be okay?"

"No Amanda, I don't trust George at all. You've seen the way he looks her up and down."

"Yeah, the same way that tattoo freak looks at me."

"Not quite, Jordan looks at you in love, George looks at LuAnn in lust. There is a big difference."

"She's in great shape. I think she could kick George's ass if he tried anything."

"Now you know why he left Mike with him in camp."

"Think that's why he sent us over for water? Just so he could mess around with her?"

"Partly yes and George doesn't like drinking boiled water from the cistern. He prefers the filtering system on the boats and it gives him time alone with LuAnn. The sooner we get back the better."

The women finished filling the water jugs and retrieved a few bottles of Richard's wine before making their way back to the shore. They secured the dinghy and loaded the heavy water containers into the wheelbarrow for the short trip back to the house. As they entered the grounds they were greeted by Mike.

"Well ladies, took you long enough."

Judy couldn't resist the temptation. "You should try it. You can work on your tan and get a little exercise at the same time."

Amanda burst out laughing at the thought of Mike in a bathing suit.

"Knock it off little girl before I drag you behind the house and teach you what big girls do."

"Touch her Mike and it will be the last lesson you'll ever give."

"You're starting to turn me on Judy. Why screw the chick when you can fuck the hen."

Totally disgusted with Mike's crude remarks the women continued rolling the wheelbarrow to the front porch of the house. Judy and Amanda carried the water into the kitchen. Through the window they could see LuAnn taking the freshly dried clothes down from a makeshift clothesline. They could see George sitting a short distance away in the shade observing her every move. LuAnn smiled at Judy and Amanda as she entered the house with an armful of clothes.

"How'd it go ladies?"

"Let's put it this way, we'd rather lug water all day than be stuck in camp with that fat asshole. How about you, any problems?"

"You mean other than listening to George's constant sexual innuendoes every time I have to bend down to pick something up? No, not really."

"Both of us have noticed how he constantly stares at you. He seems to be getting more possessive of your time. Now Mike is starting to give us a ration of shit. Between the two of them something bad is bound to happen."

LuAnn lowered her voice as she spoke, "If I had a bottle of poison we'd be out of here tonight."

Judy filed that thought away as being one possible solution to their problem.

Chapter 14

Loose Lips

Jordan had the men fan out within eyesight of each other as they began their search. They carefully walked in unison looking for any signs of a trail or other indications of recent foot traffic. Compared to the previous two days' physical workload, searching the island came as a welcome monotony breaker. The morning sun rapidly heated the islands, humid air. An hour and a half into the search Jordan called the men together for a short break.

Brandon thought this might be an opportune time to question Jordan. "How long have you known George?"

"Awhile I guess."

"How did you meet?"

"Through Mike."

"Well, how did you meet Mike?"

"At work."

It was obvious gathering intel on George through Jordan wasn't going to happen. Jordan's one or two word answers revealed little to no useful information. It was unclear if he was deliberately being evasive for fear of divulging anything that could be used against George or just wasn't much of a conversationalist.

Mark took another approach. "I let my hair grow out like yours when I was in high school. I liked the rebellious "Rage against the machine" look. I never got into the tattoos though. I guess I thought it would be too painful. Did they hurt?"

"Not much."

Well, Brandon thought, so much for taking a shot at befriending the kid.

Jordan stretched as he stood up signaling the break was coming to an end. "You guys ask too many questions."

Jordan's reluctance to answer personal questions forced Brandon into taking a completely different approach. He turned to Richard as he asked, "Judy and I were wondering how Amanda is dealing with having her life upended?"

"She's doing as good as could be expected. She misses not being able to finish her senior year."

"Did she have a boyfriend in school?"

Jordan suddenly took interest in the topic of Amanda as he reseated himself in the shade. Brandon hoped Richard understood the dynamics of why he was bringing up Amanda and what was taking place.

"No, she felt the boys at school were too immature acting."

Mark picked up instantly on what was going on. Richard was normally much too protective of his daughter to openly discuss her availability in front of a stranger like Jordan.

"So you're saying she's never been on a date?"

"I didn't say that. She went out a few times with a guy about Jordan's age."

The trap sprung. Jordan's curiosity had peaked as he joined into the conversation, "What happened?"

"Well nothing I hope."

"No, I mean did she go out with him more than once?"

Success! Jordan's infatuation with Richard's daughter had loosened up his mouth. He extended the break another ten minutes in the discussion of "Amanda this and Amanda that."

The next break proved more informative. Brandon and Mark deliberately chose to position themselves a short distance from Richard and Jordan. It would be easier for Richard to probe for weaknesses in George's grand plan by casually questioning Jordan in a one-on-one setting.

"Tell me Jordan, what's George going to do with us when the food runs low?"

"I think some of you will have to go."

"Go. Go where? With what? George has managed to remove most of our sails, solar panels, fuel and supplies. How are we supposed to get off this island?"

Jordan suddenly realized he had fucked up. Richard had successfully manipulated him into a corner. The only way they were going to leave the island would be in spirit form.

"And what about you and Mike. How long are you guys going to last when the food runs low? Are you going to have to leave the island too?"

"Forget what I said. I don't know what's going on. I think we should start heading back now. Let's go."

Though their search had failed to reveal the source of Jordan's phantom sounds, his hormones had succeeded in betraying his common sense. Distracted by a desire to gain an "in" with Amanda by making friends with Richard he had unintentionally revealed their looming fate. Jordan's attraction to Amanda could very well play a pivotal role in their escape. The best way to topple George's defenses would not come in the form of an outward attack, it would be in creating dissention from within, and watching it crumble around him.

Chapter 15

Imaginary Music

Just before sunrise the group rehashed the details of last night's roughly drawn up escape plan. Amanda would indeed play a pivotal role in their escape. The only variable was the timing. Should they implement the escape under the cover of darkness or use daylight to more accurately change the plan on the fly. Night would increase the chances of successfully getting out of camp, but then what. The prospects of being hunted down and shot on the small island would yield the same results as having done nothing at all.

Everyone agreed they would do what they had to do in order to unbalance George's control. Every gun they managed to remove from George's arsenal increased their chances of surviving by thirty-three percent.

Amanda keeping watch on the house noticed Jordan exit the door. This marked the end of Mike's task of guarding the prisoners. Jordan made his way to the shed.

"Jordan is walking this way." Amanda whispered.

Everyone quickly pulled their cushions back toward the walls leaving no sign of the tight circle they had formed during the meeting. Laying down on their beds would give no indication of the conspiracy that had taken place just minutes ago.

Jordan pulled the sail to one side as he looked into the shed.

"George wants the women to start breakfast."

"Why so early?" Judy responded.

"We usually start cooking at eight."

"Maybe he woke up hungry. I don't know."

"Good morning Jordan."

Amanda's greeting caught Jordan totally off guard. This was the first overt interest she had taken in Jordan since captivity. Not knowing how he should respond in front of the others he chose not to return the greeting. It would have been ludicrous of him to wish anyone "Good morning" under their present circumstances.

Shortly after they finished breakfast George stepped out onto the porch. It was unusual to see him holding a .38 caliber pistol. He seemed to enjoy flashing it around. The gun evidently used to symbolize his power over the group. It was also meant to represent compliance or penalty.

"Good morning people."

Evidently George, unlike Jordan, hadn't got the memo there was nothing "good" about being held against your will.

"Today I have a special treat for you guys. I thought it would be nice to eat something other than stew tonight so I'm going to send you fishing."

Whoa, Brandon thought, what's he up to. It wasn't the act of fishing that was under suspicion but rather the jovial way it was requested.

Judy exited the house carrying a number of fishing poles taken from their boats. Amanda followed with a couple of tackle boxes.

"I don't want you coming back empty handed. No fish, no eat."

As the men picked through the gear the women joined them at the table. Mark looked puzzled as he spoke, "Can you believe he's actually acting civilized this morning?"

Brandon countered, "Yeah, but you know what they say about something being too good to be true."

Richard chimed in, "Let's get out of here before he changes his mind."

The men and women started heading for the edge of the camp forcing George to yell, "No, no, no! The women stay behind. Just the men."

Benevolence comes with a price. Any joy from the act of peacefully fishing was now overshadowed by fear of leaving the women unattended in the company of George, Mike and Jordan.

It was easy to do the math. Three couples verses three horny captors with guns. In a world without law and order there was nothing to keep them from killing Brandon, Mark and Richard without fear of repercussions. They were experiencing first hand, a world now ruled by acquisition through brute force. The time would soon come when George would tire of sending the men out to do feeble chores in order to gain private access to the women. If they were going to escape this hell alive it would have to be soon.

Back at camp George and Mike were enjoying feasting their eyes on the women as they went about their camp chores. The men made no false pretenses to conceal their lust. George had ordered Jordan to stand guard over the camp as he and Mike opened up the first of three bottles of wine. Feeling secure with Jordan standing watch they began a long morning of drinking.

"They're working on the third bottle" Judy said, as she, Amanda and LuAnn continued to clean the old house."

LuAnn held up a bunch of dead plants neglected by the previous occupants. "What a pig sty."

"A pig sty fit for the pig that lives here. Kind of ironic, don't you think?"

"I think you mean "pigs that live here". Remember Mike sleeps here too."

"Thanks Amanda, you just reminded me why I wished I was wearing rubber gloves."

The women burst into laughter as Mike entered the room.

"Whazs so funny? I like to hear jokes."

"It's a girl thing. You wouldn't get it." Judy knew he would become unstable if he knew he was the focal point of the joke.

"Yeah, a gurrl thing, I get it."

"Hey, I got a funny rhyme for you girls. Camp whores doing camp chores. Whatda ya think, pretty funny eh?"

"About as funny as you in a two-piece bathing suit." LuAnn said as she burst into laughter. Luckily Mike didn't get it.

Mike's slurred speech was the first indication of him drinking one to many glasses of wine. His bloodshot eyes were the second.

"Anyways Gorge, I mean George wants you all to go into the front room. He wants to have a party."

This was the inevitable outcome the women had feared as they watched Mike and George drink bottle after bottle.

"Tell him we'll be right there. Go on, tell him." LuAnn practically shoved the fat man out the door.

As he staggered down the hallway LuAnn turned to Amanda. "Get out of the house. Take a glass of water out to Jordan. Don't worry about us. We can handle them."

As they entered the room, George lay straddled across the sofa cushions in his underwear. Mike sat across the room with his shorts pulled down to his ankles.

"Hey ladies, welcome to the party."

"What happened to your shorts?" Judy asked.

"I dunno. Itz hot. I'm hot. You look hot. Take your shorze off."

Amanda walked quickly through the room heading for the front door.

"Hey, where you going little gurlly?"

"She's taking a glass of water out to Jordan. She'll be right back" LuAnn said as she shielded Amanda's exit from George's view.

"Ain't that sweet of her. Ain't that right, Mike?"

Mike mumbled something incoherent as he slowly drifted into slumber land. This was looking like the lucky break they had been wishing for. One down and two to go.

"Listen George, why don't I open up another bottle of wine while LuAnn dances for you?"

"Thatz whut I like to hear. Letzz party!"

Judy turned to face LuAnn and silently mouthed the words "keep him distracted."

Judy could see Amanda through the front window. Amanda was doing her best to keep Jordan's attention away from the house. Judy knew she only had minutes to search through the closets and drawers of the small bedroom. Time was running out as she frantically tore the room apart looking for the gun they had seen George flashing around on the porch.

"Hurrry up with the wine!"

George was growing impatient. LuAnn had to step up the distraction as she teased him by dancing to imaginary music in her head. She seductively unfastened the top button of her shorts.

"Where's the wine bitch!" George scowled, growing more impatient as he looked toward the hallway.

To take George's attention away from Judy, she slowly started unbuttoning the top she was wearing as she continued to sexually sway back and forth. The distraction succeeded in buying them a couple of more minutes.

Judy, glancing out the bedroom window, could see Jordan walking toward the house. Despite Amanda's best effort to distract him, his sense of something not being quite right compelled him to check in on George.

"I found it!" Judy shouted from the hall.

"You finally found the wine?" George taking his eyes off LuAnn turned to look toward the hallway.

"No you son-of-a-bitch. I found your gun."

As George focused his bloodshot eyes toward the direction of Judy's voice he found the barrel of his pistol pointed directly at his head. The timing was perfect. Mike lay snoring in the chair and George was literally caught with his pants down. LuAnn buttoned up her top as she quickly took up position behind Judy. Before Judy could say a word Jordan entered through the front door.

"What the hell is going on?"

"Shoot the bitch. Shoot her now!" George yelled pointing toward Judy.

"No George, I won't do it."

The tension was definitely building.

"Judy, put the pistol down." Jordan said in a calm voice.

"No Jordan, we've taken all the shit from him we can handle. You drop your gun or I swear I'll send him to hell."

"What are you waiting for? Kill the bitch!" George ordered.

Jordan could see the rage building in Judy's eyes. If anyone was going to die it was going to be George. She had no idea how Jordan would react as she pulled the trigger.

"CLICK"

She pulled the trigger again, click... click. George burst into drunken laughter as Jordan slowly shook his head.

"You didn't think George was stupid enough to leave a loaded gun laying around for you women to find did you?"

Judy now realized why Jordan was reluctant to obey George's orders to shoot her. He knew the gun was empty all along. Judy surrendered the useless weapon to Jordan and the three women were promptly escorted back to the shack.

George was in no condition to fully realize what had just taken place. He spent the next few hours sleeping off his "good time". There was a good chance when he sobered up he wouldn't even remember what had happened. Mike, still passed out in his drunken stupor, had managed to sleep through the whole ordeal. The best the women could hope for was a little compassion from Jordan in the form of not helping to fill in the blanks of George's fuzzy memory.

Jordan had promised Amanda if George asked him what happened he'd tell him,

"You had one hellava party boss."

Chapter 16

Reflections

Around five o'clock the men returned to camp. As they entered the grounds Mark reached into the large bag he was carrying to proudly display one of the larger bonefish they had caught. The women did not react to the catch as they walked toward them. Jordan made no attempt to enforce their shack only incarceration as they approached the men.

"What's wrong Lu?" Mark asked with a serious look on his face.

"You mean besides Judy pulling a gun on George today?"

"Whoa, what happened? Tell me he's dead."

"No such luck." Judy said, continuing "George and Mike decided to start drinking wine right after you guys left. The more they drank the cruder they got."

"They didn't try to mess around with you gals did they?" Brandon asked knowing George and Mike as he did.

"Yes, and no. Mike passed out on a chair. LuAnn distracted George while Amanda kept Jordan away from the house. I tore the bedroom apart looking for his pistol."

"Sounds like you found it. What happened?"

"To make a long story short, Jordan came into the house, I pulled the trigger and nothing happened. The gun wasn't loaded."

"Don't take this the wrong way" Richard joined in "but why didn't Jordan shoot you?"

"Because he knew the gun was empty, that's why."

"Where's George and Mike now?"

"Still sleeping off George's "good time."

"What's going to happen when he wakes up?"

"Probably nothing. He was too fucked up to remember what happened and Jordan promised Amanda he wouldn't jog George's memory."

The group gathered around the table as the women retold the story in greater detail. Everyone congratulated Judy for seizing the moment and having the "balls" to pull the trigger in spite of Jordan having his gun aimed at her.

Today's events also forewarned of George's increasing desire to gain carnal knowledge of the women. They were lucky today. A sober Mike and George might not have ended with the same outcome. Everyone agreed they were quickly running out of time. Another day maybe two at tops. The rough outline of their escape plan would receive the final touches under the roof of the shed tonight.

The women decided to clean the fish and prepare what hopefully would be the last dinner on the island. As George continued to sleep it off they took advantage of his absence to create a real meal. In addition to the fish they would enjoy instant mashed potatoes, veggies and dried fruits. A far cry from George's staple of stew. Jordan sat on the porch quietly observing the table festivities. Amanda made up an extra plate and hand delivered it to him. You could tell from his reaction he was amazed and thankful for the gesture considering the circumstances.

As the women cleared the table Mark leaned in to confide in Brandon and Richard. He spoke in a lowered voice.

"Jordan didn't shoot Judy today. Jordan promised Amanda not to tell George what happened. Maybe we're miss-reading him."

Mark stood up from the table and calmly made his way toward Jordan. He kept his hands in plain sight as he closed to within 15 feet of Jordan. At that moment Jordan was the only one capable of keeping the group in check. He suddenly stood up and pointed the rifle at Mark's chest.

"Hold it. Don't come any closer. What do you want?"

"I thought you and I could have a little talk about what's going on around here. What do you think?"

"I think you need to turn around and go back to the table."

"You can't spare me five minutes?"

Jordan pulled back on the bolt chambering a round. It was a subtle way of making a point.

"OK, I see you're not in the mood. Maybe another time."

Mark returned to the table with the enlightened conclusion the only one capable of reaching out to Jordan was Amanda. It was his second and last attempt to befriend Jordan.

Twenty or so minutes had passed before George emerged from the house. Squinting through bloodshot eyes he slowly turned his head from one side to the other as he scanned the yard. He steadied his stance by holding on to one of the 4x4 posts that supported the porch roof.

"How'd the fishing go?"

The question was met with silence. The men chose not to answer for fear of expressing their opinion of what had happened in camp. They were fully aware of George's escapade and obviously he wasn't. They planned on keeping it that way.

"Come on guys. Loosen up. I know it probably wasn't as much fun as we had here at camp, but what the hell."

Mike, rubbing his eyes and looking pale, joined George on the porch. He might have had a good time drinking today but was definitely not up to par for replacing Jordan standing watch.

"Judy, why don't you be a good girl and make us a pot of coffee. Mike's gonna need it. The rest of you can go to bed."

For once the group didn't mind being told what to do. The privacy of the shed would give them the opportunity to rehearse their roles prior to tomorrow's curtain call. Mike, in his weakened condition, became a non-issue. He might actually fall asleep on duty tonight. Taking advantage of his hung over state was not in the cards. Too many variables to go wrong. Everyone agreed to stick with the original plan.

Prior to falling asleep on his cushion that night, Brandon let his thoughts reflect back on the events that had led up to tomorrow's planned showdown. What started out as a car wreck and power outage back in Palmetto quickly escalated into a life changing event. He and Judy experienced for the first time the mass chaos of a country in trouble. Their journey to this island had crossed paths with the best of humanity embodied in the crew of the "Wanderlust", which stood in stark contrast to the fate of the crew onboard "Sanity". Human goodwill and bonding among the group seemed to grow at the same pace as George's corruption and deceit.

The war of wills, whether administered through popular consensus or enforced by dictatorial brutality, has always sat at opposite ends of the scale. In a balanced black and white world even a raging storm eventually gives way to blue skies and fair winds.

Chapter 17

Reluctant Party

The group formed their morning circle hours before sunrise. Amanda was keeping a close eye on Mike sitting on the porch as they quietly rehearsed their roles. Do or die, there would be no turning back. Their surrealistic circumstances pitted the group, much like the pieces on a chess board, against an evil opponent hell bent on removing them from the board. They had one slight advantage. George didn't appear to be the type to play chess.

Nearing eight o'clock, Amanda could see Jordan leaving the house and making his way toward the shack. He was on his way to tell the women to start breakfast. He would then relieve Mike at his guard post and begin his shift watching over the men.

Breakfast proved uneventful. The group had to carefully mask the mixed emotions of nervousness and excitement as they finished their coffee. Brandon found it hard to make small talk as he tried to cancel out all the "but what ifs..." from his thoughts. The slightest betrayal of normal behavior could possibly result in forewarning their captors that something wasn't quite right that morning. Surprise was going to be their greatest advantage.

George eventually walked through the doorway and took his normal position on the porch. He looked surprisingly alert and animated. A full night's rest had erased any signs of the previous day's hangover.

"I see you guys caught a lot of fish yesterday. I suppose the girls told you we had quite a party ourselves. Oh, by the way Mark, LuAnn's one hell of a dancer."

George moved his hips back and forth as he pretended to unbutton his shirt. He was clearly trying to get a rise out of Mark. Mike stood in the doorway chuckling out loud. Mark kept his cool.

"What, no "I'll kill you if you lay a hand on her?"

Mark continued to remain silent though his eyes clearly exhibited his true feelings.

"That's okay, she's going to do more than dance for me this afternoon."

George was doing his best to antagonize Mark into a fit of rage. Any aggressive act would only aid George's desire to depopulate the males on the island.

"Fine, I knew you were a pussy. Jordan, you and Mike take these old women to the clearing behind that stand of trees and have them dig a hole for a pond. A deep hole. You can't have enough water around here."

"Pond my ass" Brandon thought. He wasn't even clever at having them dig their own grave. Their future couldn't have been more transparent as Mike slipped two clips of bullets into his cargo shorts. Their lives could now be counted down in hours.

"Grab the shovels and water bottle. It's going to be hot today. You heard the man." Mike snapped, eager to carry out George's true intentions behind the dig.

The clearing lay about three hundred and fifty feet from the house. The thick row of trees would completely hide the actions of the work detail from the house. The dirt was fairly firm and would take a few hours to excavate. Maybe longer with an unmotivated crew.

Jordan used a stick to sketch a large circle in the dirt. "Start digging along the line and work your way to the middle. Don't drag it out. George wants it done today."

Jordan took up position next to a large bush approximately fifteen feet from the circle. He pulled the brim of his straw hat forward to shade his eyes from the low morning sun. Mike sat deliberately across from Jordan. Their vantage points totally eliminated any chance of successfully trying to make a run for it.

It was an extremely hot morning. Hotter than they had previously experienced on the island. Even their guards began to sweat profusely in the shade.

Mike totally hot and miserable ordered Brandon to bring him the glass water jug. Brandon hated catering to Mike's laziness. He dropped the shovel where he stood and reluctantly made his way over to the water. As he raised the spout to his mouth to take a drink Mike shouted at him to stop.

"I didn't say you could have a drink, just bring it to me."

Brandon in a fit of rage yanked the jug away from his mouth. The force of the downward movement broke his grip on the glass container. As it hit the ground it broke into half a dozen pieces.

You could hear the rage build in Mike's voice as he shouted, "You uncoordinated son-of-a-bitch. What the fucks wrong with you."

Jordan interrupting Mike's tantrum keyed the portable VHF radio. "George, this is Jordan. Brandon broke the water jug. Could you send Amanda out with another one? Over."

A minute later George returned the radio call.

"Yeah, Amanda's filling another jug. She'll be right there in a minute and don't let Brandon break this one. How are the ditch diggers doing?"

"Good as can be expected in this heat."

"Yeah, I read ya. Hot as hell. Just make sure they finish today."

"No problem."

Richard, Mark and Brandon continued to shovel the dirt out of their own gravesite. Five or more minutes had passed since Jordan's request for water.

"What's taking your girlfriend so long?" Mike whined.

"Give her a few minutes and she's not my girlfriend."

"So you're telling me you won't care if I wanna bang her?

Amanda overheard Mikes comment as she entered the site. She walked directly over to where Jordan was sitting.

Staring directly into Jordan's eyes she handed him the jug as she spoke in a soft voice, "Water as requested sir."

"Sir?" Mike mimicked. "What about me? I'm more of a man than his skinny ass."

Amanda without showing emotion picked up the jug and walked over to Mike. With her back to Jordan she repeated the process of looking him straight in the eyes and whispered, "I wouldn't fuck you if you were the last pig on this island you fat smelly bastard!"

Amanda had succeeded in hitting his rage button. Mike reached out and grabbed her by the hair before she had a chance to back away.

"You fucking little whore.

Holding her head down by her hair he used his left hand to unzip his shorts.

"I'll show you what you're gonna suck."

Jordan sprung to his feet. Without a second thought he ran over to Amanda and whacked Mike between the shoulder blades. "What the fuck do you think you're doing? Let her the fuck go!"

"This bitch is gonna suck my cock. Back off Jordan, I'm warning you!"

Richard, Mark and Brandon stood in the ditch watching the situation escalate. Amanda continued to twist and punch as Mike started forcing her head toward his crotch.

Jordan whacked Mike again. This time using more force. The butt of his rifle firmly impacting Mike's rib cage. You could see Mike momentarily wince in pain. He released his grip on Amanda's hair and in a single motion twisted around to attack Jordan. A split second later he was swinging like a madman.

Mike's massive weight easily overpowered Jordan. Within seconds he had him pinned to the ground. His fists delivered blow after blow to Jordan's head as he straddled Jordan's chest. In an act of desperation Jordan frantically searched for anything to ward off the savage beating. His left arm was securely pinned under the weight of Mike's body. He managed to free his right hand and frantically search the small area within his reach. His fingers felt a large section of what remained of the broken water bottle. In one final burst of energy he rammed a piece of broken glass into the side of Mike's neck. Thirty seconds later the last spurts of blood signaled the end of Mike's cruel existence.

George laying on the couch was startled by the sound of two gunshots. He immediately went for the portable radio he had placed on the kitchen table.

"Where's the VHF?"

The girls just gave him a puzzled look.

"I don't know George. Where did you leave it?" LuAnn said.

George immediately ran toward the bedroom to retrieve his gun. Moments later he returned to the front room and in a panic turned his attention to an ugly old vase sitting on a shelf. He used his right arm to knock the vase to the ground revealing a box of .38 shells that had been hidden in its base. He quickly inserted one of the clips into the gun as he ran out the front door closely followed by Judy and LuAnn.

The sprint across the yard would only take seconds. He cautiously slowed as he neared the tree line.

As George and the women approached from behind they could see Jordan holding his rifle on Brandon and Richard. The two men stood near the lifeless body with their heads bowed down mourning the loss of their friend. His body lay crumpled and bloodied face down in the shallow depression.

LuAnn cried out, "Mark? Oh my god you killed him!"

LuAnn instantly broke into tears. Judy put her arm around her waist to help steady her collapsing stance.

George couldn't break his stare at the pit as he walked past Jordan for a closer look at the lifeless body.

"He wasn't much of a man anyway." Showing no signs of remorse, he smiled as he turned to face Jordan.

"Welcome to the party mother fucker!"

One shot rang out. The last two things this evil monster would ever see was Mark wearing Jordan's hat and shirt, and a .223 slug going into his head.

Chapter 18

Speed Bumps

The group stood in complete silence waiting for the piercing sound of the single shot to quit ringing in their ears. It was over. In one unflinching moment the pain and suffering inflicted on the group, both physical and emotional lay embodied in the lifeless lump sprawled in the dirt. George's reliance on Jordan and Mike to carry out his bidding enabled the group to manipulate their individual character flaws with covert precision.

Jordan wearing Mark's shirt lay face down in the hole. He slowly raised his head up. Using his arms, he pushed his body into a seated position facing the group. He kept his head bowed down avoiding eye contact as he sat awaiting his fate. Mark removed Jordan's shirt and hat and disgustingly threw them in Jordan's direction.

Luanne ran over and embraced Mark realizing he wasn't dead.

"What are we going to do with him?" Mark asked, as he kept the gun pointed at Jordan.

"Let's tie him up for now. We can decide later." Brandon replied. Judy volunteered to return to the camp to get the clothesline.

Richard requested Judy take Amanda back to the house. It was a father's way of trying to prolong having to face the inevitable reality of the new world they were living in.

"What about the bodies?" Mark asked.

"The hole looks deep enough to me." Brandon quipped as he motioned for Richard to join him.

"Help me drag Mike's body over here. The hole is shallow but we should have enough dirt to cover them up."

LuAnn, now standing near George's remains commented, "Yeah, should be just enough to keep the flies off and that's more than he deserves."

Mark and LuAnn had endured more mental torment from George than the other members of the group. His death would be seasoned with their "worst of wishes" for him in his afterlife.

Judy returned with a couple of short lengths of rope just as the finishing shovel loads of dirt were thrown. Their graves looked like two speed bumps on a car less island. There was no service, words or even an afterthought as they all silently left the area.

Entering camp, the men securely tied Jordan to the base of a tree fifteen feet from the house. The women had gathered wood to build a campfire a short distance from the shed. The fire would afford little heat for Jordan, but would aid them in keeping an eye on their former guard.

Oddly, no one seemed the least bit interested in entering the house. The house now represented the epicenter of evil in their minds. They had no reservations sleeping in the shed one more night.

As the sun set they all gathered around the blazing fire. The day's events were retold in glorious detail. Richard recapped how they were able to manipulate Mike and Jordan against each other.

"We started digging the hole. We knew we had to come up with a good reason for Amanda to join us. Brandon, right on queue, deliberately broke the glass water jug. Jordan got on the radio and presto, Amanda shows up with more water. She deserves an academy award for her part in getting Jordan jealous. Amanda won't tell me what she said to Mike, but it definitely set him off. We counted on him going ballistic and banked on Jordan coming to her rescue. While they were distracted, slugging it out, I grabbed Jordan's gun. We didn't plan on Jordan killing Mike but so much the better. Killing him quietly with a piece of glass gave us plenty of time for Mark to trade shirts and hats with Jordan. We had Jordan lay face down pretending to be dead and believe me, had he moved he wouldn't be here tonight. We drug Mike's body behind a bush, when the scene was staged we just fired two shots into the air and waited for curious George to show up. The rest you already know."

The previous night's whispered escape plan was now subject to open cheers and congratulations. It was a time of celebration among the co-conspirators. For the first time that night the group felt totally at ease on the small island. They agreed to sleep on Jordan's fate and deal with him in the morning. Though he had unknowingly played a critical role in their freedom, he would have to pay a price for his hand in carrying out George's crimes against humanity.

Around ten o'clock they decided to call it a night. Mark volunteered for the first two-hour watch over Jordan. Richard and Brandon split up the remaining watches. This promised to be the first restful night's sleep since their arrival. Promises were meant to be broken as one loose end remained tied up to a tree resulting in another restless night's sleep.

As the morning sun broke the horizon, the arduous task of dealing with Jordan lay before them. No one in the group could have ever imagined having to participate in the trial of someone they knew. Today they would truly take on the cliché role of judge, jury and potential executioner.

Jordan was moved from the tree to a chair placed at the head of the picnic table. His hands were untied but his legs and feet securely bound preventing escape. The rules of trial were simple. Each of the group would have a chance to evaluate Jordan's participation in their captivity. Everyone present could speak as much or as little as they felt comfortable with. All agreed to abide by unanimous vote. They also agreed to let Jordan speak on his own behalf. The hearing offered less than a stateside civil trial but afforded Jordan more rights than he would receive with a kangaroo court.

Richard was first to speak. "I'm not sure he would have shot us but I don't know. He certainly had no qualms about following George's orders. I mean like, would I be here today if we hadn't thrown a wrench into George's plan? Good guy, bad guy I really don't know. If you think he deserves to die I won't blame you."

Jordan showed no emotion to Richard's statement as Amanda stood to take her turn, "I don't think he's an evil person. He always treated me nice. I'm confused about him making my dad dig that hole. We don't know for sure if George would have ordered him to shoot, and if he did tell them, I'm not positive Jordan would have." She sat back down at the table.

Judy declined to comment one way or another.

Mark stood up next. "I think he would have followed George's orders to the T. I think he and Mike would have shot us without hesitation. He had no problem watching George fuck around with our women, Amanda excluded, for what it's worth."

LuAnn then spoke, "I agree with Mark. I think he's a piece of shit who would've gladly carry out anything George told him to do. I don't believe in trusting other people's feelings. Sorry Amanda, but to me he's no better than George or Mike. The world's better off without the other two and I'm not sure if it wouldn't be better off without him as well."

Brandon was the last to stand and make his statement.

"Judy and I told you about the small sailboat on the way to this island. The hull of the boat was riddled with bullet holes. The blood soaked cabin made me sick. The animals that attacked and butchered the people onboard should have to face the consequences of their actions. I will say this; I know without a doubt Jordan had a hand in the attack. I can't prove he actually killed anybody on board, but watching him parade around camp wearing a "Sanity" t-shirt proved to me he's just as capable as the other sadistic monsters who did. Jordan might have a soft spot for Amanda but I have a gut feeling he wouldn't have thought twice about putting a bullet in any of our heads.

Jordan was asked to make his statement to the group.

"All I can say is I'm sorry for following George's orders. I never thought it would come down to this. George made it clear if Mike or I didn't do exactly as we were told he'd have no problem shooting us. I know that isn't an excuse, but that's why I carried out what he wanted in order to stay alive."

Richard stood up and asked if anyone had anything to add. No one spoke. He then requested Jordan be removed from the table and retied to the tree. Richard wanted everyone in the group to be able to speak freely, unhampered by Jordan's presence, as they deliberated his involvement and subsequent penalty.

The next couple of hours were spent in a heated discussion as each member advocated for their version of "fair". Some sounding like a defense attorney pleading for Jordan's life. Others, an inflamed prosecutor demanding the death penalty. Brandon brought up the question if they decided on handing down the maximum penalty if anyone among them would have a problem taking on the roll as executioner. It came as no surprise when Mark volunteered for the job.

Jordan sat quietly in the shade of the tree he was tied to as the deliberations came to a close. A consensus was reached. It was agreed not to inform Jordan of their final decision until tomorrow.

Chapter 19

Curbside Justice

Sunrise was greeted by a thankful group of sailors. Thankful to rejoin their previous life of independent movement. Thankful to have the opportunity to distance themselves from the memory of this island, and most of all, thankful to be rid of George and his tyranny. They vowed to never fall prey to another person's power crazed visions of grandeur and "wanna be god" mentality.

The morning, as joyous as it was, would not be free of the mundane task of restocking their boats. Due to their recently gained freedom the transfer of food and equipment felt more like a privilege than a chore. They marveled at what took days to unload now looking like hours to restock. It was amazing how quickly they erased all signs of their presence as the camp started to transform itself back into the dilapidated looking farm they first entered. Replete with the rusty old tractor near the rear of the house.

A group discussion that morning to torch the house was voted down. As eager as they were to physically erase the symbol of the misery they endured, they had to consider George's story of persuading the old codgers to leave. As slim a chance as that appeared, they couldn't burn down another person's home. That said, most agreed if they had to make a wager they would have bet on their bodies being buried somewhere on the property.

Each took a short turn keeping an eye on Jordan as he sat securely tied to the tree. The suspense of not knowing the final penalty he faced must have led him to wild speculation. Each trip out to the boats and back represented a sort of dwindling count down. The men seem to enjoy the mental torture Jordan was having to endure. After all the hell he, Mike and George had dished out on a daily basis, it gave them little reason to be concerned for his feelings. Everyone knew that pay back was a bitch.

Richard, reluctant to sound like he was giving an order inquired, "What do you guys think about taking a break?"

Everyone agreed on the suggestion and sat down in the shade some thirty feet from Jordan. Amanda poured a glass of water and made her way toward him. As she got close he embarrassingly declared, "I pissed my pants."

"That doesn't come as a surprise. How long have you been tied to the tree, twenty-four hours, it could be more. The guys didn't want to run the risk of you escaping by having your hands untied." She knelt down placing the glass to his lips. He quickly drank down the water. Amanda was the first person to talk to him that morning and he was eager to learn of their decision.

"What are they going to do with me?"

"I can't tell you."

"Why not?"

Before Amanda could answer Richard yelled at her to return to the group. She gave Jordan no indication of his fate as she turned and walked back to the table.

"I think we should search the farm one more time before we leave. No one knows for sure how many guns George stashed on the property." Mark said.

"I'm sure Jordan could save us the time with a little persuasion."

Everyone knew what Richard was referring to.

"Wouldn't that be something George would have done?" Judy questioned.

"Are you thinking I meant torture? I was merely suggesting enhanced interrogation techniques."

Everyone laughed and agreed they wouldn't have the stomach to torture another person. Especially having to live with his conscience if he truly didn't know if there were any more guns hidden on the island. Their remaining time was not going to be wasted looking for illusive guns that may or may not exist.

The last hour in camp was spent gathering, cleaning and folding Richard's sails that had served as ground cover under the cushions and hung as a shed door. Satisfied everything was in order, they made their way toward the beach. Jordan was untied from the tree and escorted by a well-armed Brandon and Mark.

Never was a group of people more excited at the prospects of being reunited with their waterborne homes. Each pair launched their dinghy into the light surf. Jordan with his hands still bound was the sole occupant of George's dinghy. Mark attached a twenty-foot tow rope to pull Jordan over to the boats.

Brandon made a slow course change that set him motoring toward George's boat. As he got within 20 feet he put the rifle butt to his shoulder and began shooting small chunks of fiberglass out of the hull just below the waterline. George's boat instantly started to take on more water than its bilge pump could remove. Within minutes the once perfectly sound vessel made its way to the sandy bottom ten feet below. Only the mast and rigging protruding into the air remained visible on the surface marking the boat's final resting place. The mast and spreaders took on the form of a modern looking cross. A boat's version of a metal tombstone.

Jordan felt relieved to be returning with the group. His greatest fear of capital punishment for his involvement put to rest with each foot made good toward the boats. Perhaps in time the group would totally forgive and accept him into their fold. If he could prove himself worthy, maybe Richard would allow him to develop a relationship with Amanda. Future possibilities instantly whirled through his thoughts.

With everyone on board their respective boats the engines were started. Everyone that is but Jordan, who remained tethered to Mark's stern some twenty feet away.

"Hey, what about me? What's going on?"

"Hold tight", Mark yelled back over the noise of the diesel. " We haven't forgot about you."

The boats slowly started making way from the island. About 400 feet from shore Mark put his boat into neutral as the others slowed as well. Jordan felt relieved as Mark began pulling him toward his boat.

"For a minute I thought you were gonna leave me in this dinghy."

Mark smiled as he tossed a knife into the dinghy. "Cut your hands free and be quick about it."

Jordan awkwardly worked the knife against the rope until he was able to free his hands. Mark had made no attempt to keep the dinghy from drifting slowly away from his boat.

"Now get out!"

"What do you mean, swim to your boat?"

"No. I mean swim back to the island. The girls left you about five days' worth of food. Maybe ten if you ration it."

"What if I won't get out?"

Mark raised up his hand revealing a .45 automatic.

"If you were going to kill me why didn't you do it on the island?"

Mark took careful aim and blew a large hole in the dinghy's forward air chamber.

"You just can't leave me here!"

Mark shot again, this time deflating the starboard air chamber. Jordan realized his fantasy of the group forgiving him was just that, a fantasy. He reluctantly slipped over the remaining chamber and slowly swam his way toward the direction of the island. As he swam a safe distance from what was left of the dinghy Mark put a final shot into the remaining air chamber sending it to the bottom.

The group had handed down the cruelest, yet humane punishment they could agree on. Jordan's inevitable fate would depend on his resourcefulness as to whether he would live or die.

Chapter 20

South

As the boats raised their sails, not one among the group looked back at the small island. The overhead sun illuminated the crystal clear water under their keels as the boats took on a triangle formation. Brandon and Judy once again enjoyed Sparrow under full sail. The gentle rhythmic motion of weaving through the small swells became hypnotic, if not intoxicating.

The steady afternoon breeze created all the energy needed to propel Sparrow comfortably along at her maximum hull speed of six knots. Judy, basking in the sun lazily kept her hand gently on the tiller using minimum pressure to hold course. The best remedy to wash away a bad memory was the mix of clean air and warm wind.

At this moment no one seemed to mind aimlessly sailing with no particular destination in mind. They seemed to relish in the simplicity of the moment. Soon enough their uncertain future would force them to return to reality, but for the next few hours they didn't seem to care.

Eventually their elation, as comforting as it was, would have to be replaced by having to start making plans for surviving in an alternate reality.

"What do you think is happening back in Palmetto?" Judy asked.

"Probably not good. I read once as much as seventy percent of the people would die in the first year of a national catastrophe."

"I think your figures are wrong."

"Maybe, hell I don't remember for sure but imagine trying to survive in a world without food, electricity or drinkable water. How long do you think the population is going to last?"

"I agree; a lot of people are going to die. Especially the older ones. I'm not sure I would want to live in a Mad Max world."

"Sweetie, you're living in one now. The only difference is we have a way of trying to find a third world country that has learned to survive most of those hardships. We might end up in a country that's ruled by a corrupt government, but what the hell, aren't they all?"

"Agreed, they're all pretty much the same."

"Besides, look at all the people trying to survive on welfare and still going hungry at that. We've really become a dumbed down nation totally unequipped to survive in the real world. Too much dependence on bureaucrats designing our lives. Like Reagan said, "Government isn't the solution, government is the problem."

"Okay, at our age what are we going to do for work? Do you really want to have to start learning a foreign language? I know I don't."

"Yeah, me either. Nobody said it would be easy. Look at it this way, we're sailing off on a grand adventure."

"Kind of like what we just left?"

"Well, we survived the first round didn't we? And even at our age. I think of it as a good experience."

Judy had to laugh as only Brandon would categorize events that took place on the island as "good experiences."

"Man, what I wouldn't do for a cigarette right now."

Judy silently took it back. The fact that Brandon was forced to quit smoking was an exception to all the bad things that had happened.

"Where did you stow that shortwave radio?"

"Don't try to look for it you'll never find it. Take the helm, I know where it is."

A couple of minutes later Judy entered the cockpit with the small radio. Handing the radio to Brandon she once again resumed control over the boat. Brandon attached the wire antenna and crossed his fingers...

"Let's hope we have better luck this time."

The garbled noise of a distant radio transmission started blaring from the tiny speaker.

"I wish this thing had a better tuner."

Judy watched as Brandon hovered over the small radio. She subconsciously used her fingers to twist the ends her hair.

"What do you expect for thirty-nine dollars? You get what you pay for."

Between what sounded like Morse code, a barely discernable conversation in a foreign language, static, static and more static, Brandon quickly lost patience and tossed the radio overboard.

Judy couldn't resist commenting, "Great, now you're going to take your frustration out on the fish."

If they were ever going to find out what was happening outside their watery world it would have to come from another source.

"Start a new wish list, first on the list buy a better radio so the next time the world falls apart we'll know what's going on."

As the late afternoon wore on, the conversation centered on the positive lessons they had experienced. One, there is safety in numbers, two, carrying a weapon to protect yourself isn't a bad thing and three, don't trust strangers and finally four, don't join a group ruled by a dictator. Failing to follow the four golden rules had nearly cost the men their lives.

As the sun began to set Richard's voice came over the VHF radio.

"Well, what do you guys think? Where do you want to go?"

A few seconds later Mark answered back. "LuAnn and I don't care. Anyplace is better than where we were."

"OK, one vote for anywhere. What about Judy and Brandon, any suggestions?"

"Well, we were thinking at some point being stuck in hurricane alley is going to bite us in the ass. If we found a terrific little island around here we would still have to move come June. We suggest heading south, preferably to a good hurricane hole."

"Sounds like your suggesting somewhere near Panama? Ecuador? Venezuela?"

"Anyone of those destinations works for us." Mark remarked.

"That sounds good to me as well. We'll have to sail south past Cuba, unless you guys want to go north and cross over near Miami again."

Richard was right. There was only one real choice.

"South." Cued Mark.

"South." Brandon added.

"South it is. I'll set a southerly heading and let you know what it is. Everyone stick together."

Judy went below to make a new entry in Sparrow's log book. She filled in the date and time. Pausing to contemplate what to enter into the third bracket the answer suddenly came to her, Destination: Unknown.

Chapter 21

Going Where?

The following morning found the sea shimmering with small teal colored wavelets as a steady breeze gently nudged Sparrow along a southerly heading. Judy maintained a safe distance from Mark and Richard's boats as the small convoy enjoyed spectacular sailing conditions that morning.

Brandon, turning to Judy asked, "How's she steering?"

Judy knew it wasn't a random question. Correct sail adjustment to the force and direction of the wind would reduce the amount of pressure Judy would have to apply to the tiller to maintain course. The goal was to steer with as little effort as necessary.

Judy momentarily took her hand off the tiller to demonstrate how balanced the boat was sailing. "She's handling great. Very little pressure needed to keep on course. How are the batteries doing?"

Brandon entered the cabin to check the battery monitor. Without the luxury of dockside a/c power, the batteries were now solely dependent on the solar panel to keep charged. Thirty-seconds later he popped his head out the companionway to report, "House battery topped off and motor batteries fully charged."

With everything under control Judy's thoughts turned to fixing them something for lunch.

"If you want to take over steering, I'll make us something to eat."

"You got it." Brandon said as he traded places with her at the helm.

The small swells gently raised and lowered Sparrow as the lazy late-morning wore on. The VHF radio broke the peaceful serenity.

"This is Richard. How are you guys doing back there? Over."

"LuAnn and I are doing fine," answered Mark, adding "Can we pick up the pace a little? Over."

"That depends on Sparrow." Richard replied trying not to laugh.

"What's the rush Mark? Judy and I are enjoying cruising along at a relaxed pace. Besides, Richard hasn't picked out a destination yet. What's the point in speeding balls out without a specific direction to steer to? Over."

Richard cut in, "I'm still working on it and, Brandon, maybe you could sheet your sails in a little tighter."

"Fine. How fast do you guys want to go? Seven knots? Eight knots?"

Mark keyed his mic still laughing, "Sparrow doing eight knots in this breeze, dream on."

"Okay, how about five?"

"If that's the best you can do Brandon aren't you risking a nose bleed at that speed?"

"You're a funny man Mark. Over and out."

"It's great to hear Mark laughing," Judy said.

"I agree. I thought he might end up a little messed up after killing George."

"Messed up for killing George? George pushed him way beyond the point of having any sort of guilty feelings."

"I won't argue with that. One lesson George taught all of us is to be careful with who we let in the group. From now on we have to totally trust and feel comfortable with new people that want to join us."

Brandon adjusted the main and jib sheets increasing Sparrow's windward speed by another knot.

Brandon and Judy were aware that the warm tropical waters and mild breeze they were enjoying could turn wicked at the drop of a hat. Having recently weathered a treacherous storm helped reinforce the need to keep a constant eye on Mother Nature.

Sparrow's forty-five-year-old rigging and sails had recently been replaced, but an old boat by its very nature is just waiting for something to break down. In a world that now lacked parts for repairs, the smart thing to do was try to minimize the stress on the boat and hopefully stave off inevitable breakdowns as long as possible.

As the day waned, the clouds eventually created a beautiful sunset. The colorful flaming yellow gave way to fiery red billows that slowly transformed the vivid colors into drab gray. With the last remnants of useful light starting to dissipate in the West, the stars slowly made their nightly appearance in the eastern sky.

"Have you seen my sextant? I want to get in a little practice shooting the stars and get a fix on our position."

"Why, think the GPS is going to go down?"

"I don't have any idea how long it's going to continue to function. It doesn't hurt to practice and, besides, I just like shooting the stars."

"I'll get it for you, you'll never find it."

Judy was right, he never paid attention to where she stowed things on the boat.

"You need to hurry, I have to see the stars and the horizon at the same time and we're losing that window."

"Why didn't you think of looking for it earlier?"

Brandon snapped back, "Forget it, I don't want to put you out. I'll find it tomorrow."

"Sounds to me like you're getting into one of your moods."

"I'm just tired of never being able to find where you stow things inside the boat."

The stress they had endured since leaving Palmetto was starting to have an adverse effect on Brandon's temperament. A welcome pattern interrupt came as you could hear Richard's voice hailing the boats over the radio.

"Listen up guys, I think our best bet is sailing toward Panama."

After what seemed like a long silence, Mark's voice came over the radio.

"That's quite a distance from here skipper. Over."

"Yeah, I estimate about 1,100 miles."

Brandon cued his mic to add, "Why Panama, you couldn't come up with anything closer?"

"It's one of a few places we can avoid hurricanes and stay safe."

Mark rejoined the conversation. "So I take it you're thinking about having us sail between Cuba and Haiti? Over."

"Yep, then we'll swing past Jamaica and we're home free. Over."

Brandon expanded the area on his chart plotter to view the proposed route.

"The gap between Cuba and Haiti looks to be about fifty miles wide. Are you comfortable sailing that close to shore? Over."

"More comfortable than choosing the alternate route; sailing between Miami and Cuba. Besides, I don't think any of us are really up to backtracking to the North. If you guys have any suggestions I'm all ears. Over."

Mark agreed with Richard's choice, "Panama works for us. Over."

"Judy and I agree as well. We just seem to be sailing farther and farther from home. Over."

"That's true, but what choice do we have. We don't know what's going on back in Florida and from what we've come across, I sure as hell don't want to stick around here to find out."

Mark adding, "We can't hang here very long anyway. I don't know about you guys but I don't want to be caught here during the hurricane season. Over."

"That's not for another six months. We just hate to be sailing farther away from our son each time we move. Over."

"I understand what you're saying, we all have family back in the states. I have no problem turning around and heading back the minute we hear people aren't killing each other in the streets. Over."

Mark adding, "Good luck with that."

Mark's sarcastic remark to Richard's statement embodied how easy civilization could slip into a barbaric mindset with little provocation.

Richard continued his analysis of the proposed route to Panama. "Okay then. We have about a hundred and fifty miles before we enter the pass between Cuba and Haiti. I know I don't have to say this, but keep your eyes open for other boats. I don't think we'll have any problems with the Haitian's, but if we come across the Cuban military that might end up another story. Over."

"Speaking of Cuba, any chance we can just sit it out in their country?" Brandon asked.

"If they give us the same kind of welcome we gave the refugees fleeing Cuba when Castro took over, definitely not. As far as the Cuban authorities go, if we're stopped, we're heading for the Canal Zone and have no intentions of making landfall on their soil. Over"

Brandon ended the conversation with one last question, "What do you have in mind when we get to Panama?"

"We're just going to wing it when we get there. We've got a lot of water to cross before that happens, so stick close together and don't lose track of each other. The barometer seems to be holding steady so I don't think we'll see any major change in the weather tonight. That being said, it's still unpredictable tropical waters. Richard out."

There was nothing more for Brandon and Judy to do but prepare for a comfortable night's sail. They discussed the order of two on, two off watches they would keep. The moon was rising late in the evening and would aid their ability to keep track of their companions in the dark.

Tomorrow Richard would issue emergency rendezvous coordinates in the event one or more of their boats became separated from the group due to adverse weather conditions.

As Sparrow gently rolled back and forth to the rhythm of the wind, Brandon and Judy had no way of knowing the ever increasing challenges they would soon encounter as they slowly sailed into the night.

Chapter 22

Detour

The predawn hours found the group sailing close to Inagua Island, the third largest land mass in the Bahamas. Rich in lore and heavily documented with historical fact, the island had witnessed many a treasure filled Spanish galleon unintentionally finding its final resting place on the sandstone shoals.

"This is Richard, are you guys listening out there?"

Judy and Mark responded to Richard's hail over the radio.

"In an hour or so we're going to be nearing the entrance to Mathew Town Harbor. It's located on the southern tip of that island lying off our port side. The chart says the lighthouse is active, but I didn't notice it blinking. My question is what do you think about going into the harbor? I think we should try one last time to find out what's happening in the states before we totally commit to Panama."

"This is Brandon. What's the island like? Over."

"Listen Brandon, I can recognize all your voices over the radio. I know its protocol to say 'over' but let's get real. Unless you guys have a problem I say we drop the 'over and out' stuff."

"I don't have a problem dropping it." Brandon replied.

"What say ye, Mark?"

"Whatever." Adding, "Are we going to be taking a chance the local officials will try to impound our boats if they find out we have weapons onboard? Some of these islands have a strict 'no gun' policy."

"I don't think that's how it works. I figure the worst thing they can do is not grant us access to the island. We really don't know how far south the power outage has affected other countries and, with the light house being out, something tells me we better go in armed. We'll just keep the guns hidden until we know what's going on. So is everyone in agreement?"

"We're game." Brandon answered back.

Mark adding, "Count us in as well. What else do you know about this place?"

"From what Amanda read from our cruising guide, it's a decent size island with a population of around 900 people. A majority of the population works on the other side of the island at the Morton Salt yard. What makes the island unique for this area is a large fresh water lake. I think, if I remember right, she called it Lake Rose or Rosa... something like that."

"What's the big deal about the lake?" Mark questioned.

"It doesn't mean much to us because we purify our own water supply. Boater's having to depend on natural sources would find the further south they sailed, the harder it would be to find drinkable water."

"So you're saying this island is going to be like a magnet for refilling empty water tanks."

"Put it this way Mark, it's definitely going to be one popular watering hole if this area doesn't get much rain this year."

Fifty minutes later the small armada tightened formation as they approached the entrance. Their weapons carefully concealed but at the ready should the need arise.

Under normal circumstances the group would have radioed port officials in Mathew Town after anchoring their boats. Flying their yellow quarantine flag they would patiently wait for the local customs official to do a quick inspection, fill out paperwork and grant access to the island.

Richard's voice came over the radio, "How about a change in plans. I think a couple of us guys should go in alone to check things out. The rest of you can anchor out here until we radio you to come in."

"Splitting us up is kind of risky don't you think." Mark replied.

"I figure a single boat will draw less attention entering the harbor. If the island is friendly, no problem. If it isn't, no need to put all of us at risk."

"This is sounding less and less like a good idea." Judy said to Brandon.

"Much as I hate to admit it, I have to agree with Richard. I'll go with you."

"Thanks Mark. Amanda can stay with LuAnn. I'll have her take the dinghy over to your boat and you can take it back to mine."

Their plan was to stay in contact by radio. Should trouble arise, it would be up to Brandon and the women to come to their rescue.

Having safely anchored the boats outside the harbor, Mark motored over to Richard's boat. Once onboard, Mark pulled back the bolt on his rifle chambering a round. He clipped a small portable VHF radio to his waist band before turning to Richard saying, "I'm ready Skipper, take her in."

The early morning sun made it difficult for Richard to see very far ahead as they neared the main anchorage inside the harbor.

Five hundred feet from shore, Mark noticed a half inflated dinghy floating 50 feet in front of them. Richard slowed the boat down as they closed the distance.

Mark straining to see through sun squinted eyes suddenly called out to Richard, "Stop the boat! There's a girl inside the dinghy."

Richard's boat came to a stop alongside the small weather beaten inflatable boat. Mark quickly concealed his rifle in the cockpit locker before leaning over the rail to help her climb on board.

The woman in her twenties gave Mark a big smile. Her sun bleached blond hair, oversized sunglasses, hot pink shorts and provocative Polynesian t-shirt radiated 'tourist' on every level.

"How long have you been floating out here and why so close to shore?"

"About ten minutes."

"Ten minutes? I don't under..."

Before Mark could finish his question, the young woman pulled out a small caliber pistol she had managed to conceal under her shirt.

"Step back, sit down and don't move." She said in a stern voice. She then used her left arm to signal someone on the shore.

Mark sat down next to Richard.

"Does this trick work every time?"

"I wouldn't know, you're the first boat we've tried it on. Men are such suckers. Poor little girl drifting all alone in a boat."

Mark having doubts as to her ability to actually pull the trigger, started to stand up.

She pulled the hammer back chambering a round.

"Sit back down or kiss this world goodbye!"

Mark and Richard had been duped by a simple ruse. The young woman had deceitfully played the role of a young damsel in distress, but the tone of her voice when it came to pulling the trigger, conveyed a message of total sincerity.

Chapter 23

Control Freak

The young woman held Richard and Mark at gun point as a small dinghy with two male occupants slowly rowed toward them.

"I see you're not alone."

"This is the last time I'm going to tell you to shut up!" she ordered, giving Mark a threatening look.

It took a few minutes for the dinghy to make its way over to their boat. The front passenger secured the dinghies painter to a cleat on their starboard side. Both young men appeared to be unarmed as they climbed aboard Richard's boat.

The taller of the two men stood next to the young woman.

"Nice work Trish. So what do we have here, a couple of wannabe hero's?"

"Looks that way. I told you it would work. I got us a boat. Now, can we get off this shitty island?"

"Yeah, you had a great plan to hijack a power boat. I don't recall you saying anything about a sailboat. Do you know how to sail? I know Marty and I don't."

"Give me a break, how hard could it be? Pull the sail up and just steer like you're driving a car."

"I don't think it works that way. I have a suggestion, let's take the older one with us until we know what we're doing."

Obviously, Richard's slightly graying hair qualified him as the 'older one'.

It wasn't hard for Richard to tell the trio lacked experience when it came to hijacking boats. "If we run into bad weather, it's going to take two people that know what they're doing to keep this boat floating."

"Give me a break. What's the worst that could happen?" Trish seemed to be a master at emphasizing disagreement just by the sarcastic tone of her voice.

Richard countered, "Well for starters, the mast could break, the boat could roll over and if you're lucky enough not to drown, you could swim around waiting for the sharks to finish you off."

"I don't think you want to die in a storm any more than we do grandpa."

It suddenly dawned on Richard that Trish was calling all the shots for the trio. He had one more incentive to try to keep Mark on board.

"You didn't let me finish. There's a lot of water out there. If you don't know how to navigate this boat with pin point accuracy, you could just keep on sailing never finding land. You're going to eventually run out of food and water. Not a pretty way to die."

"I think he has a point Trish." Marty, the shorter man said in agreement.

Trish hesitated for a few seconds before asking, "What do you think Don? Should we keep both of them on the boat?"

Without hesitation, Don answered back. "Hell no, I agree with you Trish. He doesn't want to die of thirst or hunger any more than he wants to drown in a storm. I say we have the other guy row back to shore and we get the hell out of here. It's a lot easier keeping an eye on one of them than two."

Don motioned Mark to get off the boat and climb into the dinghy.

"Is there anyone else in town?" Mark asked just before going over the side of the boat.

"Not in town. They all went inland to the lake. They're afraid people with guns will come into the harbor looking for food."

"That's enough talk." Trish scowled. Marty obediently dropped the conversation as Mark reluctantly began paddling toward the shore.

"I'm going below to find something to eat. Don, you keep a close eye on the old man."

As the boat aimlessly drifted in the harbor Trish, Don and Marty helped themselves to the food stored below. They gorged the food down like they hadn't eaten in a week. Five minutes later they all went topside where Trish ordered Richard to set sail.

"Before we shove off, I need to check the gauges in the navigation station."

"Why?" said Trish in her distrustful questioning tone.

"I need to make sure the battery is on and the knotmeter and depth sounder switches are working. You don't want to run aground on a sandbar do you?"

"Don't you have to just raise the sail?" Trish inquired.

"No. The first thing I need to do is check the sail systems before we can point the nose into the wind. Then we the raise sails."

"Fine, just be quick about it. Marty, keep an eye on him down there."

Richard's bullshit story gave him an excuse to enter the cabin. Richard sat down at the navigation station and went through the motion of checking gauges and flipping switches. Marty paid little attention to Richard's movement as he sat slumped back at the table contently digesting his food. Richard covertly switched the cockpit mounted VHF radio fuse to the off position. The last thing he wanted was Trish to pick up on radio transmissions between their anchored boats that were hiding just outside the harbor entrance.

Stepping into the cockpit Richard said, "Okay, I think we're ready to shove off."

Mark successfully reaching the shoreline took up position behind a four-foot brick wall concealing his actions as he unclipped the radio from his belt.

"This is Mark. Richard and I screwed up. We fell for a dumb ass trap."

Within seconds Brandon came back over the radio. "What kind of trap?"

"Let's just say they're keeping Richard hostage on his boat and made me row to shore."

"How many onboard?"

"Four, counting Richard. Two guys and a girl. All in their mid-twenties."

"What kind of weapons do they have?"

"One handgun."

"You've got to be kidding, right? What about your rifles?"

"They don't know the guns are there. I hid them in the cockpit locker. Look, we were stupid. Let's just leave it at that. They're going to try to leave the island on Richard's boat."

"What makes you think they won't hear us on the radio?"

"Richard knows I took the portable radio with me. Hopefully he'll find an excuse to turn off the one on the boat. If he doesn't, well it really won't matter. You're going to have to rescue him regardless."

"What are they like? Hardcore? Amateurs?"

"Definitely amateurs."

"Any suggestions?"

"Yeah, come at them with both boats. When you get close start firing near their boat. Believe me that's all you'll have to do to take the fight out of them."

"Sounds like a plan."

"Oh, and Brandon don't trust the girl, she's an innocent looking evil bitch."

"Got it. Are you okay? Where are you?"

"I'm fine. According to those kids, the townspeople abandoned the town to go inland. I'm hiding near the main pier."

"Okay, we'll get back to you as soon as we can."

Amanda and LuAnn kept close watch for Richard's boat near the entrance to the harbor, while Brandon and Judy maneuvered Sparrow directly across from their position.

They didn't have to wait long before Amanda broke the radio airwaves catching sight of her dad's boat.

"They're coming. Looks like under sail."

"Amanda, be careful. Try to shoot close to the boat but don't hit it. If they don't surrender right away, I'll take a few shots at the cabin. We don't want to accidentally shoot your Dad."

Richard continued to steer a course toward the center of the entrance to the harbor. Two or three minutes had passed before he caught sight of the other two boats closing in on his position.

"It looks like those boats are coming straight at us." Trish yelled back to Richard.

"They're probably just looking for a safe anchorage like we were."

"No, they look like they want to sandwich us between them." Trish's voice conveyed a slight twinge of panic.

"Let me try to contact them on the radio."

"Go ahead old man. Tell them to stay away from us."

"I'll need you to hold the wheel for a second while I go down below to switch the radio on."

Trish reluctantly took control of the wheel while Richard went below and quickly flipped the switch on.

Reentering the cockpit, he again took control of the wheel with one hand as he brought the mic up to his mouth with the other.

Trish repositioned herself alongside Richard. "Be careful what you say old man or your dead."

"Two boats approaching dead ahead, state your intentions. Over"

The hail was met with ten-seconds of silence. Trish ordered Richard to call them again.

"Two sailboats approaching dead ahead, state your intentions. Over"

As Sparrow closed within 150 feet Brandon's voice came over the radio. "Drop your sails and prepare to be boarded."

"What do you want me to say Trish?" Richard asked as he silently enjoyed watching her squirm for an answer.

"Tell them to fuck off and leave us alone. No wait, tell them we're armed and we'll shoot anyone who tries to get on this boat."

Richard starting to enjoy the game keyed the mic, "The captain says she'll shoot anyone who tries to board us."

Brandon retorted with, "Wrong answer it's your funeral."

Judy and LuAnn continued to close in on Richard's boat while Brandon and Amanda took careful aim. Within seconds they unleashed a barrage of bullets in Richard's direction deliberately hitting the water near the boat.

The radio suddenly sprang to life as Trish yanked the microphone from Richard's hand realizing she was seriously out gunned.

"Stop! Stop! Stop! Quit shooting! We give up!"

Richard quickly pointed the sailboat directly into the wind stalling their forward motion, as Marty and Don stood with their hands in the air. Brandon and Amanda kept their rifles pointed at Trish and her crew.

"Are you all right Dad?" Amanda yelled from her position on Mark's boat.

It took Trish about three-seconds to realize she still maintained bargaining power.

"Dad? You old son-of-a-bitch." She quickly spun around pointing the small pistol directly at Richard.

"Back off or he's dead. I'm not kidding I'll blow him away."

Brandon without thinking twice slowly squeezed the trigger letting one bullet fly, fatally striking Trish in the chest.

Chapter 24

One Way Trip

The rag tag group of marina neighbors that left Palmetto less than a month ago, were quickly learning the ins and outs of what it took to stay alive in the lawless world they now inhabited. Every stranger they encountered would have to be considered dangerous until proven otherwise.

Don and Marty were transferred to Mark's boat where LuAnn cut a couple short lengths of rope and quickly tied their hands behind their backs. Having securely bound the two young men alongside the mast, LuAnn started the motor for the short trip into the anchorage closely followed by Brandon and Judy on Sparrow. Richard volunteered to sail about two miles offshore and unceremoniously dump Trish's lifeless body overboard letting the current take her remains where it may.

Finding a suitable depth in the harbor, LuAnn dropped the anchor while Mark, leaving his hiding place near the end of the pier slowly paddled his way toward his boat. Twenty minutes later Richard entered the harbor and anchored his boat nearby. All gathered on Mark's boat to decide the fate of the two young men.

"What's their story?" Brandon asked.

"All Mark and I know is the girl mentioned being stuck on this island and wanting to leave. I say we let Mark go forward and question them."

"What if they won't talk?" Mark said with a slight smile.

"I have a feeling you won't have a problem getting information from them. Check out how nervous they look."

Richard was right. Both men appeared extremely distraught as they sporadically twisted from one side to the other trying to catch a glimpse of their captors.

Mark slowly walked up to the young men seated on the deck near the mast. Without saying a word, he pulled the slide back on the .45 semiautomatic pistol chambering a round. The unmistakable sound of impending doom let the captives know how serious and potentially lethal their interrogator could be.

"How long have you guys been on the island?"

The shorter of the two spoke first.

"We've been here about four weeks."

"How'd you get here?"

"A friend of ours chartered a cabin cruiser boat..."

The taller one started to speak, "Yeah, some friend he..."

"Shut up! Let your buddy continue." Mark snapped.

"He had this great vision of the ultimate grand adventure. All of us were having a good time when we first got here."

"How many of you were there?"

"Five in all. Me, Don, Trish, Marla and Keith. Keith's the one who chartered the boat. The second day on the island things began to unravel."

"What do you mean unravel?"

"We partied hard the first night we got here and didn't get around until eleven the next morning. Keith and Marla had been listening to the radio on the boat that morning and told us to go ashore and bring back ice for drinks. At first we thought they were just wanting time alone. We motored the raft over to the beach. Everyone seemed panicky in town. The shelves of the main store were empty. I mean like nothing left on the racks. Don, Trish and I decided to go back to the boat but when we got to the beach we noticed Keith, Marla and the boat were gone."

"So you don't know what triggered the panic?"

"Not really. Later that day some people from the salt refinery showed up in a rush to leave the island. We don't know what they said because the people in town wouldn't tell us, but whatever they said definitely made the locals go crazy. An hour later there wasn't a person left in town."

"How have you guys managed to survive a month without food?"

This time Don, the taller one spoke up.

"Trish has, I mean, had a way of getting what she wanted. You saw how clever she could be. I mean she almost got away with stealing your boat."

"So you're saying she talked the locals around here into giving you food? I find that hard to believe."

"Let's say she knew the people living in the Bahamas weren't allowed to own firearms. On the trip over here, she flashed a gun she brought aboard bragging nobody will ever come between her and her .38."

"So she stole what she wanted at gunpoint?"

"Pretty much."

"So neither one of you know what triggered the panic? You didn't hear anyone mention problems back in the States?"

"No. We thought the problem was local. Why? What's happening back home?"

"Nothing any of us can do anything about. You guys are better off staying here until things settle down in the states. I suggest you try kissing up to the locals. Oh sorry, I guess that won't work thanks to Trish's little armed robbery stunt."

"Couldn't you take us with you?"

"Take you where? Hell, we're not exactly sure where we're going. Besides, if we took everyone we came across that's stranded, or out of food and water we would need a ship the size of the Titanic."

"So what are you going to do with us?"

"That's what I'm about to find out." Mark made his way back to the cockpit to discuss the severity of their punishment.

The group wanted to know the outcome of Mark's questioning and were disappointed to learn the two young men knew less than they did.

Mark opened with, "What are we going to do with these guys? I think I'm speaking for all of us when I say I'm not looking forward to holding a trial every time we come across scumbags trying to steal our shit. There has to be a faster way to dispense justice."

Richard wasn't quite sure what Mark meant by 'faster way'. "So what are you suggesting? Put a bullet in their heads? Granted, I think people like George and Mike who tried to kill us on the island and Trish who tried to hijack Richard's boat deserve a bullet in the brain-end of story. I don't feel Jordan and these two fit in the same category."

Judy broke into the conversation. "The way I see it, there's a paper thin line dividing them from us. Right now we're not worrying about where our next meal is coming from. We also have a damn good form of transportation to get around on, but let's be real, it isn't going to last forever. One of these days we're going to be forced into making the same kind of decisions these two guys were forced into. Is trying to stay alive by any means wrong? Do those two warrant, no let me back up, do any of us warrant a death sentence for just doing what we have to do to stay alive?"

"Yeah, yeah, I get what you're trying to say. So tell me Judy, where do we draw the line? What justifies killing and what qualifies release? I assume that's what you're getting at."

"I think we all know what justifies shooting someone, Mark. I think we should just let them go."

Mark turned to face the rest of the group. "Everyone agree with Judy on just letting them go?"

Everyone shook their heads in agreement.

"Okay, let me handle this." Mark said, as he again walked over to where the two men were sitting.

"We've decided to let you go. I want you to know one thing before I untie you. If you try to interfere with us in any way, shape or form while we're here, you're going to earn a one way trip offshore, just like your friend Trish. Do I make myself clear?"

Both men shook their heads in agreement.

"Now get off the boat and swim to shore. I don't want to see your faces again."

As the men dove off the boat, Mark turned with a smile on his face and walked back to the rest of the group.

"One way trip offshore? I like that." Amanda said, adding, "We sound real bad ass." Everyone burst into laughter.

The group was slowly developing a way to balance adrenalin inducing moments with the levity of laughter in an insane world.

Richard brought up a question for Mark. "Did you see anybody moving around town from where you were hiding?"

"Not a soul. I mean no dogs, cats, people, nothing."

Richard adding, "Those kids told us everyone in town went inland. They said they were afraid people would enter the harbor by boat and try to take away what little food they have. Can't say I blame them."

LuAnn, who had been quietly listening suggested, "Well, if the town's deserted like they say and Mark didn't see anyone moving around, I think we might consider setting up guard watches on the boats and spending the night here in the harbor."

"Good idea LuAnn, I agree." Richard added, "The next leg is going to be a long one to Panama, at least seven to ten days of open water sailing. I suggest we take advantage of the layover to make sure the boats are ready for the crossing."

Judy had been carefully studying Brandon's uncharacteristic somber demeanor since Trish's death. "Are you okay Brandon?"

"You mean after having to shoot the girl?"

"Yes, how are you doing?"

"To tell you the truth I don't know. I didn't mean to kill her. I was aiming for her shoulder but the boat was bobbing around just enough to throw my aim off."

"You did what you had to do. I think she was crazy enough to pull the trigger on me." Richard said, as he gave Brandon a nod of approval.

Mark tried to ease Brandon's conscience. "If it helps, I didn't feel bad after I shot George. Think of Trish as George's evil step sister and I agree with Richard, she was definitely capable of pulling the trigger."

Chapter 25

Items of Opportunity

Everyone returned to their boats and began closely inspecting the rigging, sails, propulsion, food and water for the upcoming Caribbean Sea crossing.

With nonexistent weather forecasting, luck would definitely play a role in making a successful crossing.

Forty-five minutes into the process of checking their boats, Mark's voice came over the radio. "I've got a small problem, the hose to my water tank is leaking. I need to replace about four feet of three-quarter inch hose to the pump. Anybody have any extra hose onboard?"

"I don't think so but I'll look." Richard replied.

Brandon radioed back, "Can't help you Mark. We carry a few backups but ¾" hose we don't have. Can you tape it?"

"No way. Whoever the idiot was who installed the hose cut it off to the exact length and it's leaking just past the clamp. Even if I could I don't think it would hold up very long. That's if it worked at all."

Richard returned to the radio. "Sorry Mark. All I found is a two-foot piece of 1/2" hose I saved for under the sink."

"Thanks for looking. Anybody have any ideas?"

Richard thought for a moment before suggesting, "What do you think about going ashore and trying to scrounge up a piece of hose that will work? I don't know how much fuel you've used up but it wouldn't hurt to see if we could round up a few more gallons of diesel while we're at it."

"Works for me Richard. When do you want to go ashore?"

"How about four this afternoon. That will give all of us a chance to see if we need anything else."

"Sounds good. I'll meet you on your boat at four."

"Wait! I want to join you guys. Sparrow's water is down five gallons and I wouldn't mind topping off before we cross."

"Down five gallons? How big a tank does Sparrow have, or should I say how small?" Mark commented.

"Thirty gallons forward and another twelve-gallon tank connected to the cockpit freshwater shower."

"You've got to be kidding. I carry about 120 gallons and I imagine Richard carries about the same. What the hell are you doing way down here in such a small boat?"

"We all made it to the same place, didn't we? Judy and I know how to conserve water when we have to. Technically Sparrow is thirty-two feet from stem to stern, only five feet shorter than your 'bigger' boat."

Richard joined in, "He's got a point Mark. I think Sparrow was originally designed as a day sailor not a coastal cruiser, so far I'm impressed."

"What about those guys we set free? What if they decide to come back to the boats once we're on shore?"

"Are you kidding, Mark? The way the girls worked together as a team against George and Mike, you couldn't help but feel sorry for those guys if they tried. Besides, they can radio us in plenty of time if they see anyone coming."

Amanda, taking the mic from her father's hand, confidently stated, "Dad's right. We can take care of ourselves."

Mark's impending water tank problem gave added incentive to double check all the primary systems onboard.

Besides fuel, hose and water, the final scavenger list included toilet paper, soap, sunscreen and small assorted batteries. Other than the hose the other items could have been classified as a wish list.

At four o'clock Richard climbed into his dinghy and motored over to pick up Mark and then Brandon. Mark and Richard made room in the cramped dinghy for Brandon's two five-gallon plastic jerry cans he would use to transport water back to his boat.

As the three set course for the shore you could hear the women wishing them "good luck" and "be careful" except for Amanda yelling "Don't forget the toilet paper!"

Chapter 26

Right or Wrong?

As the dinghy approached the shoreline Richard pulled the emergency stop on the small noisy outboard motor. The sudden stillness in the air created a high pitched ringing in their ears. What lay before them was the surrealistic look and feel of an abandoned ghost town.

"Make sure the safety's off on your guns." Mark whispered as they made their way toward the nearest building.

Amanda tried her best to keep track of the men with binoculars. LuAnn kept watch on the entrance to the harbor while Judy, facing the opposite direction, scanned the nearby shoreline.

The men slowly approached an aging old dilapidated hotel.

"Let's split up. I'll go in the front. Brandon keep an eye on the rear entrance. Richard, you keep watch for anybody coming down the street. Make sure of your target. Don't get jumpy and shoot one of us."

Mark silently entered the lobby that recently welcomed tourists from all points of the globe. This wasn't just a hotel; it was more than likely some sort of landmark on Inagua.

Several minutes passed before Mark reappeared at the rear door motioning Brandon to enter the building.

"Amanda, do you copy?"

"Yes, Mark, loud and clear."

"We're inside the green and white building."

"Affirmative. I saw you go in the front door."

"If you gals see anything moving let us know."

"Will do."

"Start looking around for anything we can use. Don't waste your time upstairs, I've already checked up there. The rooms are stripped clean; they even took the toilet paper."

The inside of the building looked remarkably unmolested considering the town's hasty evacuation. The two story aging hotel was the second tallest structure on the island, only topped by the lighthouse. A large ornate chandelier hanging from the tall ceiling definitely went along with the overstuffed furniture in the lobby, but looked out of place on a tropical island. After a few minutes of checking the main lobby and coming up empty handed Mark suggested, "We need to find a hardware store or a general store."

As Brandon exited the hotel he handed Mark a tourist map that provided points of interest and the approximate location of various businesses located along the waterfront. "I think this will help."

"Where did you find this?"

"Laying in plain sight on the main counter."

Mark quickly scanned the small tourist map desperately looking for a hardware store. "The map shows one down this street two blocks on the right side."

Mark once again radioed Amanda. "We're going to check out a hardware store about two blocks east of this building. Keep an eye on us as long as you can."

"I don't think I can see that far down the street. There's a building blocking my view."

"Do the best you can. I'll get back to you when we reach the store."

Mark turned to Richard and Brandon. "Keep a safe distance from each other. Let's go."

Carefully scanning the surrounding area, the men cautiously moved down the street.

A few minutes later Mark radioed the message they were about to enter the store.

The sign over the door read 'Martinez Hardware'. The rustic appearance of the building displayed that lay back 'island' look. Reality quickly returned as the door lock showed signs of forced entry. Entering the small business, they found various items littering the floor. Anything of any real value had recently been removed. The hardware section or, what was left of it, yielded little to no help.

"What the hell, no hoses or clamps?" Mark's voice was starting to take on a tone of desperation.

"What about the black hose out front connected to the water faucet? It looks to be about three quarters in diameter."

"How in the hell did I miss that? Thanks Brandon. You guys see if you can find anything useful while I liberate a hose."

Brandon had to laugh as he turned toward Richard holding one of the few large items left in the store. "Have any use for a weed whacker?"

Richard didn't pay attention to Brandon's attempt at humor as he continued to comb through miscellaneous odds and ends that heavily littered the isles of the small store.

"Give it up Richard. We're wasting our…"

Brandon stopped mid-sentence. "This is what Judy was talking about."

"Talking about what?"

"I was just thinking, what if the owner of this store came in on us right now. Aren't we stealing his property? Would we blame him for wanting to shoot us?"

"What are you getting at?"

"Nothing, other than Judy was right. Only a thin line separates us from what we consider bad people and, the way I see it, that line is getting thinner every day."

"What are you guys talking about?" Mark asked as he reentered the store with a four-foot section of hose.

"Brandon's wanting to spark a philosophical debate over the definition of right and wrong."

"Seriously Brandon, you want to grow a conscience right now?"

"I wouldn't call it a conscience. I just think..."

The radio suddenly erupted with, "I see movement on the street. Repeat guys, movement on the street."

Chapter 27

Consequences

"How many and where?"

"I count seven heading in your direction from the area of the first building you were in."

"Are they armed?"

"You broke up, say again."

"Are they armed? Do they have guns?"

"I can't tell. Could be rifles. Could be sticks or clubs. Whatever you guys are going to do, you better do it fast."

"Got it. Stay off the radio, I don't want it to give our position away. I'll get back to you."

"Does this place have a back door?" Mark was obviously wanting to avoid a confrontation.

"Yeah, it does. Unfortunately, it's on the side of the building their coming up on. We'll be in plain sight if we try to go out that way."

Richard's information eliminated all but one option.

"We're going to have to hunker down in this building. I don't want to shoot anyone if we don't have to but, if they fire on us, I'm going to aim to kill and I suggest you guys do the same."

The three men took up position near the storefront window and doors. They arranged their bodies to be able to keep an eye on the street without giving their positions away.

"Here they come, stay cool." Mark whispered.

What started out as muffled noise slowly transitioned into the distinct sound of young voices.

"What the hell." Mark whispered. "It's a bunch of teenagers heading this way."

Mark discreetly peered out the window. "They're not armed. A couple of them are carrying baseball bats."

Richard whispered back, "What are we going to do if they see the boats in the harbor?"

"You're right, I'm going to have to create a distraction." He propped his rifle against the wall and stood up. "Cover me, but don't let them see you."

As Mark exited the doorway the teenagers stopped in their tracks.

"What's up guys? Going to play a little baseball?"

The oldest looking kid spoke for the group as they positioned themselves in a semi-circle formation facing Mark.

"Where'd you come from? I don't remember ever seeing you around here."

"I've been here awhile. I don't remember seeing you kids either."

"We're not kids. A couple of us are almost seventeen. Do we look like we play with marbles? I don't buy your story about being here awhile either."

"What are you trying to say kid?"

"I think you're here stealing stuff."

The tension was starting to rise. The group's body language was beginning to take on a more aggressive posture.

"I don't like being called a liar!" Mark snapped back.

"Then what are you doing in my uncle's store? Christmas shopping?"

Mark's decision to distract the teenagers from noticing the boats anchored in the harbor was not going well.

One of the older boys motioned the others to form a circle around Mark. "I think we need to teach this thief a lesson."

Along with the baseball bats a couple of kids suddenly brandished small knives, further escalating the tension.

Brandon and Richard were forced out of their concealment to come to Mark's rescue. Stepping out of the door with weapons at the ready, Richard demanded in a voice two octaves lower than he naturally spoke, "Back off and freeze!"

The commanding adult voice resonated with the teenagers, they froze in their tracks.

Mark walked toward the direction of the doorway to retrieve his gun. The circle of teenagers parted giving him ample room to pass.

"What the hell's wrong with you kids? Do you want to be shot? Not every..."

Before Mark could finish, one of the younger boys broke from the circle and furiously ran down the street while the others instantly cheered him on.

"You're in trouble now. Wait till he tells our parents you're holding us at gun point."

Another one adding, "You've got about fifteen minutes to get out of here and go back to wherever the hell you came from."

Having made no attempt to shoot at the fleeing kid the others realized the men with guns weren't going to shoot them. Gunshots even fired in the air would lead to them having to deal with an angry mob of parents converging on them from all directions.

"Go on, get out of here. All of you leave." Mark ordered.

The kids no longer felt the momentary fear from the intruders and only backed up a short distance.

Mark clutching his gun and four-foot section of hose in his left hand used his right to contact Amanda on the radio.

"This is Mark. Get the boats ready to leave, and I mean now!"

As the three men beat a hasty retreat toward the beach the teenagers continued to follow, picking up rocks and other small objects.

Reaching the dinghy, Mark, Richard and Brandon placed their guns on the floor of the small boat before dragging it into deep enough water to start the engine. The teenagers started to throw rocks and anything else they could get their hands on.

Richard yanked half a dozen times on the starter rope but the engine refused to start. Rocks began to pelt the water with increasing force as the teens moved ever closer to their intended target.

"I don't know what's wrong with the motor! It ran perfect on the way over." Richard said as he continued to pull on the rope.

Brandon reached for his rifle. "Those kids are going to end up hitting one of us in the head if we don't get out of here fast. You sure you don't want me to scare them off with a couple of shots over their heads?"

"Hell no." Mark replied, "The townspeople will think we're shooting at the kids if they hear gunfire."

Brandon continued to duck as the menacing rocks flew past. Trying to think of a reason why the outboard motor wouldn't start, he asked Richard, "Did you snap the red plastic kill switch back on the throttle?"

Richard paused for a moment as he reached into his pocket and removed the red piece of plastic. "Sorry guys, in all the confusion I forgot to attach it." Two pulls later the small motor sprang to life. Within seconds of shifting the motor into gear the boat steadily moved away from the shore and safely out of rock throwing range.

Richard motored Mark and Brandon back to their boats.

"I guess you must have really pissed those guys off." Judy commented as she continued to scan the beach.

"For starters, those guys are just a bunch of kids and, yeah, I guess you could say that."

"Don't take this wrong, but are we really running from a bunch of snot nosed brats?"

"Not exactly, one of the little punks went running back to where all the townspeople are hiding. You know, the supposed nine hundred people that live on this island. He can't wait to tell their parents how we held them at gunpoint."

"Yes, I could see where that would present a problem."

Richard's voice came over the radio. "We better move outside the harbor before the townspeople get here. The opening at the entrance is a little too close for comfort."

Judy had been scanning the teenagers on the shore when movement in town caught her attention. "Here they come, looks like a mob of a hundred or more people heading toward the beach."

The angry shouting from the shore, made the decision to leave a very wise choice.

Minutes later the boats were floating far enough from shore to minimize the immediate threat from the townspeople.

Chapter 28

Off and Running

"Well, that was cutting it close." Brandon remarked as Judy maneuvered Sparrow out of the harbor.

"Next time you guys go on a shopping spree try not to get run out of town."

"Just keep an eye on following Richard, I'm going forward to hoist the sails."

Brandon struggled raising the mainsail. Normally Judy would have pointed Sparrow into the wind making his task easy. Turning into the wind now would have meant hanging a U-turn directly back toward the angry mob.

After much yanking and straining on the mainsail halyard he successfully raised the sail into its proper position. Next Brandon loosened the jib furler lines and with little to no effort watched the two small jibs instantly unfurl and fill with air. Turning to face Judy he was surprised to find her sitting at the helm smiling at having raised and adjusted the small mizzen without his assistance. "Looks like you have everything under control. I'm going below to get out of the wind and radio Richard."

"I'd rather you used the handheld radio out here. I can't reach the mainsheet, if I have to spill the main."

Judy was right, the wind had been steadily building in velocity as the afternoon wore on. If the wind continued to intensify, a sudden gust could easily threaten to broach Sparrow without warning. From her position sitting behind the mizzen mast, she wouldn't have enough time to reach the mainsheet if she had to quickly spill the air out of the sail.

Retrieving the radio from the cabin Brandon keyed the mike. "I take it we're heading toward the Windward Passage?"

A few seconds later Richard radioed back. "I don't see where we have much choice."

Mark joined in on the conversation. "I checked the distance on the plotter. If we can continue to maintain six knots, we'll be there in about eight or nine hours."

Brandon glanced down at his watch. "It's six now. That means we'll be shooting the passage about two or three in the morning."

"That time of night is going to give us a slight advantage." Richard replied.

Richard's response puzzled Brandon. "Slight advantage? How so?"

"For one, the Haitian's are more than likely not to have radar and, two, they'll probably be asleep at that hour."

Mark injecting, "I think if I had a choice, I'd rather run into the Cuban military than Haitian pirates."

"I'd rather not run into either one of them. The darkness should work in our favor avoiding the Haitians."

"What about the Cubans?"

"There's an international treaty regarding major straits separated by countries. Let's just hope the United States is still able to maintain the strength it needs to enforce those rights."

In Richard's closing statement, he had managed to bring the great unknown to the forefront. The group had adequate food and fuel to continue into the future. What they didn't possess was a clue as to what was going on back home.

The prevailing northeast wind, blowing twenty knots, put the wind on their portside beam for the next fifty miles. The strong wind guaranteed a wet and wild ride as the boats rolled from one side to the other as the waves slowly but steadily increased in height.

Their primary objective lay before them; enter the Windward Passage. A narrow fifty-mile-wide opening that separated the Atlantic Ocean from the Caribbean Sea, and unfortunately for the group, Cuba from Haiti.

"I'm going to go below to make sure everything is staying secure." Brandon said.

"Don't take too long. I need a short break when you're done."

Brandon quickly checked that no loose objects were bouncing around in the interior of the boat. He found it increasingly hard to move around without holding on to stationary cabinets and other non-moveable parts of the interior to keep his balance as the waves continually tried to bounce him from one side of the boat to the other.

Exiting the cabin Judy hollered, "Well, what do you think?"

"I think we should change Sparrows name to Maytag."

Judy was too tired to smile at Brandon's joke.

"Why don't you radio the other boats and find out how their doing."

"I thought you wanted a break?"

"I do, but I can wait a few more minutes."

"Yeah, I agree, it doesn't look like this wind is showing any signs of wanting to ease up."

Having weathered a couple of nasty storms since leaving Palmetto, Brandon and Judy were not looking forward to another sleepless night.

"You know sweetie, weather like this makes me dream of a dry bed on land. The only thing that keeps me going is knowing the wind will eventually quit blowing and things will return to normal."

Returning to Judy's request he wedged himself in the companionway opening to minimize the noise created by the wind and cued the transmit button on the portable VHF.

"This is Sparrow. Repeat. This is Sparrow. How are you guys doing?"

Mark was the first to reply, "So far so good. Had a hell of a time installing that short piece of hose. They never give you enough room to work on a boat. How are you and Judy doing?"

"We're okay. Everything is still staying glued together."

Amanda broke into the conversation. "Dad and I are doing okay. I hope this wind doesn't blow as strong as the last storm we sailed through."

"I'll second that." Mark said in agreement.

"Good, we just wanted to check in on you guys before the sun sets. Sparrow Out."

They all knew rendering assistance in this wind during the day would be tough. Rendering assistance once the sun had set; nearly impossible.

Chapter 29

Anchors Aweigh

The early evening hours continued to provide a steady 25 knot wind. Brandon and Judy had wisely elected to put a double reef in the mainsail. The three small boats kept a safe distance from each other maintaining a rough diamond shape formation. Richard, taking on the role of mother duck, didn't mind getting on the radio to remind the ducklings to tighten formation at the first sign of straying out of place.

As darkness fell, the sound created by the wind whistling through the rigging was only rivaled by the swishing sound of water cascading and splashing in defiant resistance to the boats forward movement.

The state of the sea continued to worsen. Any hope of comfortably passing between the two land masses that night wasn't going to happen.

As close together as Judy and Brandon sat in the cockpit, the building wind made communicating with each other increasingly more difficult by the hour.

"Well, Judy, it looks like we're in for a rough night."

Judy thinking out loud mumbled "I think I have a harder time with the noise the wind makes than I do the waves."

"It doesn't bother me until it starts moaning. I don't mind the whistling sound it makes passing through the rigging, but when it starts that low moan you know you're seconds away from getting slammed."

Two hours later Amanda's voice hailed the two boats over the radio.

"My dad wants me to give you emergency rendezvous coordinates in case we get split up tonight. Let me know when you're ready."

It took a minute or so for Judy and Mark to grab a pencil and something to write on.

"This is Judy. Ready."

"This is Mark, go ahead Amanda."

"19 degrees 19 minutes north, by 17 degrees 33 minutes west. Dad says we should stay off the radio until we're clear of the passage."

The evening was much cooler that night forcing Judy to go below and find her windbreaker for the evenings overnighter.

During the evening Brandon and Judy periodically traded positions at the helm so the other could try to grab an hour of sleep. Unfortunately, the rough water had reduced that dream to settling for uneasy rest.

Having carefully studied the chart plotter Brandon and Judy knew once they entered the passage they would have to try to sail the next ten miles directly down the center. They both understood it would take at least two hours before they would have the opportunity to veer away from the main traffic lane and safely enter the Caribbean Sea, hopefully undetected.

Nearing the center opening to the passage, Judy, following Richard and Mark, slowly turned Sparrow onto a southwest heading. The change in direction gave a little relief from the constant rolling motion of gusting wind and waves on the beam. Brandon readjusted the sails accordingly.

The next two hours would keep the group on high alert as the passage promised to be the greatest obstacle to date.

"How are you holding up Sweetie?"

"I'm doing fine. How about you?"

Brandon was too keyed up to even think about feeling tired. "I'm doing great. I'm surprised we don't see any lights coming from Cuba or Haiti from here. Two countries I've never had a desire to visit."

"I didn't think we would see lights this late at night. I would have liked to have visited Cuba under different circumstances."

"How much further do we have to go?"

Brandon checked the distance on the chart plotter. "Looks like another seven miles to clear the channel. Should take us about another hour or so."

"What's our speed?"

"Feels like a steady six knots. Why?"

"The wind feels like it's stronger than that."

"It just feels that way because we changed direction."

Brandon knowing Judy preferred verification glanced down at the knot meter.

"We're moving along at... 7.2, you're right, it's definitely blowing harder. I think we better drop the main and just fly the mizzen and jibs before the wind gets any stronger."

"That works for me, the double reef is still having too much sail up in this wind. You know we broke a cardinal rule."

"What rule?"

"If you wait until you think it's time to reduce sail…"

"I know; I know; it's too late."

Brandon knew bringing down the mainsail would be no easy task as the wind continued to overpower the small boat. He snapped one end of the safety tether to the built-in harness on his lifejacket and the other to the jackline which was securely attached to fittings located fore and aft on the deck. Judy snapped her tether to the jackline as well. If either of them were to accidentally fall overboard, the tether and jackline would keep them securely attached alongside the hull until they could be pulled back onboard.

Judy moved slightly forward to let the mainsail out as Brandon positioned himself near the base of the mast.

"Let it go!" He shouted.

Judy released the mainsheet which let the sail take a position much like a flag looks blowing in the wind. The upside was by reducing pressure on the sail, Brandon would have an easier time letting it slide down the narrow channel in the mast that held it upright in place. The downside was the un-nerving noise made by the loose end of the sail violently snapping in the wind.

Having successfully lowered the sail, Judy pulled the mainsheet taught centering the boom to the boat. Brandon quickly gathered in the limp sail as best he could by gathering it on top of the boom and attaching small lines to hold it in place. Not an easy task as the boat violently rolled from side to side.

Hanging on to the handrail Brandon carefully observed the timing of the oncoming waves. Waiting for just the right moment he quickly made his way back to the safety of the cockpit.

"Well, that was fun."

Judy knew he was being sarcastic. "Well 'Mister Good Time', how about taking the helm while I go below to pee."

Brandon had to laugh. "Good luck in this weather."

Luck was right. Everything below deck was securely fastened, secured or screwed in place. Nothing would move except the curtains swaying with the waves. Trying to find a secure position to brace yourself while you sat on the head was another matter. It was all you could do just to go below in rough weather and keep yourself from being tossed around like a tennis shoe in a clothes dryer.

Like most resilient sailors Judy had managed to complete the task at hand looking no worse for wear as she reentered the cockpit.

"How's she handling?" Judy now had to shout over the wind and waves.

"Good as can be expected considering..."

Amanda's voice suddenly blurts out over the radio.

"We're in big trouble! Repeat, we're in trouble. Dad slipped and fell in the cabin just after cutting a line in the anchor locker. He thinks he broke his arm when he fell."

Mark instantly came back over the radio. "Why did he cut the anchor line?"

"A big wave hit us and ripped the bow roller mount from the deck. Dad says, if we don't let the anchor loose it's going to end up swinging around and gouging a hole in the hull large enough to sink us. He wants me to go forward and release the chain on the windlass. He's having a tough time steering with one arm. Wish me luck. Over."

The storm had managed to scatter their group out of visual range of one another.

Judy, Brandon, Mark and LuAnn shared the frustration of having to stand by their radios for updates which meant the only type of assistance they could render came as moral support over the radio.

"You can do it Amanda, just make sure you're harnessed in. Remember, one hand for the boat, the other for yourself."

"Thanks Judy, stand by a minute, dads trying to tell me something. I can't make out what he's trying to say over all the noise out there. I'll be right back."

A few seconds later she rekeyed the mic.

"Dad says if you don't hear back from us in ten minutes something went wrong. I got to go, Dads waiting."

Amanda clipped her harness to the jackline as the sound of the twenty-five-pound anchor swinging like a clapper in a bell continued to assault the fiberglass hull with each passing wave.

"Remember, all you have to do is go forward and release the chain on the windlass. Did you grab a knife?"

Amanda pulled her lifejacket up just high enough to expose a rigging knife securely clipped to her waist.

"If we get knocked down by a breaking wave just hang on. If we roll over and stay upside down release yourself from the harness. If you have trouble with the carbineer opening up, cut the safety strap with your knife. "Are you ready?"

"Hell no Dad." She shouted as she reluctantly stepped out of the cockpit and onto the deck.

"This is crazy." Amanda thought as she slowly started to make her way forward.

"HANG ON!" Richard yelled, just seconds before a large wave collided with the beam of the boat.

Using both hands to hang on to the wooden handrail bolted along the cabin top, Amanda closed her eyes and braced for impact. The violent motion nearly dislodged her footing from the deck.

Richard shouted as loud as he could over the fury of the storm, "IT'S HARD TO HOLD HER STEADY! WAIT UNTIL I TELL YOU TO MOVE FORWARD!"

Richard knew they were floating on borrowed time. Failure to free the swinging anchor would result in catastrophic damage to the hull near the waterline. Within minutes of bashing a hole in the side of the boat, it would take on more water than the bilge pump could handle, ultimately sending their floating home to a watery grave.

"GO FOR IT!" He yelled, calculating she had just enough time to go forward and wedge herself in the metal framework of the bow pulpit before the next wave struck.

The remaining two boats anxiously monitored their radios for news of Richard and Amanda's success. Ten minutes turned into fifteen and still no word. LuAnn tried to desperately make radio contact over the next forty-five minutes as the possibility of losing two close friends began to slowly become a possible reality.

Chapter 30

Sunset Tomorrow

The predawn light of morning gave way to calmer weather as the wind storm lost its intensity. The steep waves would take a few more hours to gradually return to a more manageable state.

Brandon and Judy, much like Mark and LuAnn, spent the next couple of hours coming to grips with the probable loss of Richard and Amanda. An aimless crisscrossing search pattern by two boats over such a wide body of water would have been futile. Both boats agreed over the radio to meet up at the emergency rendezvous coordinates Richard had issued and let fate control the outcome.

Brandon kept a constant watch along the horizon for any signs of Richard and Amanda as

Judy held Sparrow on a steady course for their destination.

"We're closing in on 'X' marks the spot. I'm surprised Mark hasn't beaten us here." Brandon mused, as he continued to scan the area with binoculars. "The storm must have blown them farther off course than us."

"No sign of Richard and Amanda?"

Brandon gave Judy an incredulous look. "Do you really expect to see them waiting here for us?"

"You don't know for sure they went down."

"You sound like you don't think I care. Believe me Judy, I care. Nothing would make me happier than seeing them again. I'm just trying to stay focused. You have to accept the possibility they didn't make it through the storm."

"You are planning to stick around here long enough to give them a chance to show up though, right?"

"You're starting to really piss me off. Of course we will. I'm going to go down below and grab a short nap. Wake me when Mark shows up and don't let me sleep more than thirty minutes."

"Aye-aye, Captain."

"Whatever."

Judy knew Brandon's short temper was the result of the possibility of losing close friends, physical exhaustion and lack of sleep. The intensity of the storm may have passed but, the byproduct left behind had manifested itself into uncharacteristic personality traits, least of which came as diminished civility. Nothing she knew a couple of hours' rest couldn't correct.

Brandon had no sooner dozed off when Judy reluctantly had to summon him back on deck.

"Wake up. I see Mark's boat coming this way."

A minute later Brandon emerged from the cabin.

"How long was I out?"

"About fifteen minutes."

Judy held the portable VHF radio close to her mouth. "Any sign of Richard and Amanda?"

Thirty-seconds later LuAnn radioed back. "No sign of them or their boat."

The remainder of the day was spent aimlessly drifting within the proximity of the rendezvous area. Having dropped their sails and aided by the light to non-existent breeze, made keeping sight of each other an easy task. One person would nap while the other kept an ever watchful eye on the horizon for any sign of Richard's boat.

As the sun set in the late afternoon, what little hope still remaining for a successful reunion with Richard and Amanda diminished even further. Neither boat had brought up the inevitable question of how long they were willing to wait. As darkness fell, Mark radioed Brandon and Judy.

"I'm thinking we should give them one more day."

"Yeah, that's what we were thinking too."

"The weather seems to be holding. I say if they don't show by sunset tomorrow, we continue on. What do you think?"

After a short pause Brandon came back over the radio. "That works for us. Hopefully the breeze will pick up and we'll have a comfortable sail tomorrow night."

Chapter 31

Jimar

As the sun broke free of the eastern horizon the long night's vigil came to an end.

Judy enjoying a cup of coffee, rechecked the slowly diminishing food supplies while Brandon made a routine inspection of the sails and rigging.

"Looks like she's no worse for wear. The furler line is starting to chafe a little near the drum."

"Meaning?"

"Meaning we need to keep an eye on it. How are we doing on food?"

Judy paused for a few seconds before responding. "Let me put it this way. I think we'll have just enough to get to Panama. Just to be on the safe side we better start thinking about catching fish."

"You're kidding; our supplies are getting that low?"

"That depends on how often and what you want to eat. How many times have I told you we better start fishing?"

"At two meals each a day, we probably have about two weeks. We're not going to be eating veggies until we make Panama, that's why I want you to start dragging a fishing line behind us."

Two hours later found Brandon sitting in the shade of the mainsail with fishing pole in hand. As he readjusted his butt that kept falling asleep on the hard deck, he noticed something unusual off in the distance.

"Judy, grab the binoculars."

"What do you see? Do you think its Richard and Amanda?"

"I don't think so, too small. Check it out. What do you think it is?" Brandon stood and pointed toward the boats eight o'clock position.

Judy quickly tried to readjust the focusing wheel which was set for Brandon's poor eyesight.

Before she could tune in on the floating object, LuAnn's voice came over the radio.

"Do you guys see that? Whatever it is it's coming toward us."

"Yeah, we see it too. Judy's having a tough time making it out."

"Mark thinks it could be a person trying to catch our attention. We're going to motor over and check it out."

"Remind him what happened last time he tried to rescue someone in distress."

"I think he learned his lesson, he just cocked his gun."

It took Mark and LuAnn about five and a half minutes to motor over to what appeared to be a worn out inflatable dinghy with two of the three air chambers inflated. Its sole occupant was a 'thirty something' tall Haitian looking man with wild dreadlock hair.

LuAnn placed the boat in neutral some ten feet away from the stranger.

The dark skinned man spoke with a thick Jamaican accent. "You are an angel my friend. I have been stuck in this leaky raft for two days without water."

He quickly raised his hands in the air as Mark trained the barrel of his pistol at his head.

"Do not shoot mister. I am a gentle person."

"What are you doing way out here?" Mark said in a demanding voice.

"I will tell you everything I know but we must leave this place. It is not safe here."

"What do you mean not safe? We've been here a day and a half and haven't seen anyone but you."

"There are bad people in boats patrolling this place. They look for people to take things from. They are not nice. They are not like you. Can you spare a little water? I'm very thirsty. It's been …"

"Yeah, you told me, two days."

Mark stepped closer to LuAnn and whispered, "What do you think? Should we take him on board?"

"He might be able to tell us something about what's going on in the states."

Mark returned to his original position facing the dark skinned man.

"Can you swim?"

"Yah Mon. I am a very good swimmer."

"Good. Swim over to the ladder and come aboard."

Mark handed LuAnn his gun.

The lanky man seemed to struggle near the top of the ladder forcing Mark to help him get on deck.

"The woman is going to keep the gun trained on you. I wouldn't recommend you try anything funny. She is a very good shot."

"No problem Boss Mon."

"I'm not kidding, one false move and your dreadlocks will be wondering where your head went."

"You won't have any trouble out of me Boss Mon."

"Quit calling me Boss Mon. My name is Mark and the woman with the gun pointed at you is my wife LuAnn."

"It is nice to meet both of you. My name is Jimar."

LuAnn radioed Brandon and Judy of their decision to rescue the 'mysterious' floating guest.

She handed the gun back to Mark before going below deck to gather food and water for their weather beaten guest.

"I see you are two boats together. That might be why you haven't been attacked. The bad people like boats all alone that don't put up a fight. Do you have more guns?"

"You ask too many questions. How do we know the 'bad people' didn't send you out here to spy on us?"

"I only ask because I don't want to end up in another leaking boat out here."

"Let's just say we don't have a problem defending ourselves."

"That is good to know. Where are you...?"

"ENOUGH! I'll ask the questions. How did you end up floating out here in that piece of crap?"

"I was a crew person on my brother-in-law's motor boat. We left Haiti heading to Jamaica and got caught in the storm. The motor quit working and a large wave made us roll over. The only thing left floating was me and that rubber boat."

"Who else was on the boat?"

"We were four. My sister, her husband and child." Jimar's eyes began to tear-up as he recanted in vivid detail the harrowing story of losing family members to a dark and angry rolling sea. Mark and LuAnn could tell from the Haitian's emotional state he was telling the truth. LuAnn tried to comfort his anguish. "We feel for your loss. It's looking like we may have lost close friends during the storm as well. It was a father and daughter. They had problems with their anchor that had broken free and it was violently hitting the bow of the boat. Richard, the father had broken his arm below deck cutting the anchor rode in the anchor locker. That left his daughter, Amanda, to go forward on deck to release the chain, setting the anchor free. They were supposed to radio us when it was done. We never heard from them again. They weren't blood relatives but they were family just the same. They were supposed to meet us here if we got separated. We're going to give them another six hours to show up before we move out."

"What kind of boat do they have?"

"The hull is dark blue and the top white. Why, did you see another sailboat out there?"

"It was too dark to see the color and I did not see a sail. It motored pretty close to me and I waved and yelled but it kept going."

"Was an old man at the wheel? LuAnn asked, raising her hopes?"

"Give it up LuAnn. We have to face the fact they didn't make it or they would have met us here."

"Not a man, it looked like a young woman steering."

"I thought you said it was too dark to see?"

"The light from the cabin was shining out on her as the boat passed by me..."

Chapter 32

Back To The Beginning

"Brandon, Judy, pick up the mic."

"Go ahead LuAnn. What's the story?"

"We'll let him tell you his story later. He just told us he saw a boat last night with a young woman at the wheel."

"That's awesome! Which direction was the boat heading?"

"That's the tricky part. He's not sure. He said the boat was moving under power doing about 4 knots."

"Why didn't they stop to help him out?"

"Jimar actually seems like a decent guy, but I could see Amanda freaking out at the sight of his wild dreadlocks flying in the breeze. He could scare the hell out of anyone crossing paths with him in the dark."

"I see your point, I also forgot about Richard's arm. Are you going to try to find them?"

"Yes."

"Do you want us to stick around here in case they show up, or join you in the search?"

"We definitely should stay together. Jimar says they have local wannabe pirates running around terrorizing defenseless boats along this stretch."

"No problem. We'll keep you guys in sight, just in case these local pirates try to give us a hard time."

"He says if they think you're willing to put up a fight they'll leave you alone."

"Isn't that the way pirates have always operated?"

"Yep, something like that, anyway, here's what I'm thinking. The breeze has been slowly picking up this past hour. Jimar says they passed him at a slight angle off his port side which would put them on a higher heading than the direction his raft was drifting. I have a feeling Richard and Amanda lost their electronics last night."

"That would make sense why they didn't meet up with us. We better head out. There's only about six hours of daylight left."

Mark and LuAnn had a hard time devoting their attention to the search with so many unanswered questions to ask Jimar. The country he was fleeing from was hardly affected by events transpiring back in the states. The fall of one or more super powers was of little interest to impoverished countries beyond the fear of an all-out nuclear holocaust created by the madness of enforcing a mindset of mutual destruction.

"So tell us Jimar. Do you know what is happening back in the United States?"

"It is not good. My brother-in-law heard Chinese soldiers have been seen gathering in large numbers on your western shore and as far inland as Colorado and New Mexico. Colorado is a state isn't it?"

Mark and LuAnn instantly stopped scanning the horizon.

LuAnn focused her attention on Jimar. "Yes, Colorado is a state. Do you know what and who started this whole thing?"

"You know nothing? You must have been sailing these warm waters when it started."

"No." Mark countered, "We left Florida two days after the grid went down."

"You are very lucky my friends and smart."

"I don't know if I would call it lucky or smart. Just tell us what you know."

"At first no one knew why your power source went off. There was little information in the beginning. Slowly word got out over the shortwave radio of people killing people over food. Not just where you come from, but all of America. We thought a country as strong as the United States could just quickly fix the problem and everything go back to normal."

"How did the rest of the world react?"

"No one came to help America. My brother-in-law said he thinks other countries were too scared if they helped it would happen to them next."

"You mean Europe, Australia, and the rest of our allies just stood back and let it implode?"

"I do not know if they tried to help or not. If they did, I don't think they were successful. All I heard on the radio with my own ears was someone say America was on her own."

"Didn't the government try to restore order?"

"If they did they were not successful."

"What about the military? We have one of the largest in the world. Couldn't they control the people?"

"I feel the most sadness for your soldiers. They were stationed on military bases in countries all over the world. Unfortunate for America, she could not get enough of them home in time to help her own people. Now they say those that are stranded will have to find their own way back."

"Then what happened?"

"Then the radio went quiet. We listened for five days and did not hear any news. I fear many, many people died during that time."

"How long ago was it when the radios went quiet?"

"I think about four weeks ago. Maybe five."

"Tell us about the Chinese? When did you hear about them landing on American soil?"

"We were told of this last week. People say the Chinese started a cyber-attack that shut down your electrical poles."

"You mean the grid."

"Yes, that's what they called it. Power grid."

"If they're not transmitting on shortwave radio how do you know about the Chinese invasion?"

"News of America travels slowly. We get information from people leaving your country by boat and sometimes small airplanes. Most are on their way to Central America."

"No one tries to transmit on shortwave anymore?"

"The radios only pick up static. People say the signals are jammed. Maybe China. Maybe Russia."

"Russia? Why do you think the Russian's would jam the signal?"

"Everyone is talking about the two remaining super powers trying to lay claim to as much American property, as they can, before a treaty is drawn up. I feel very sad for your country."

"So you're telling us the Russians are occupying the East coast?"

"Yes, they are using the shipping ports on the East coast to stockpile military equipment for future base settlements."

"Son-of-a-bitch! I can't believe the U. S. would just quietly stand by and let two fucking countries invade our shores."

"It is hard to stop an invasion when there is no one there to stop them."

"I can't imagine how we were caught off guard that bad, and I'm amazed the Chinese were gutsy enough to carry out another Pearl Harbor type attack so easily. Their element of surprise has to be wearing a little thin by now. I guarantee the American's still alive are armed, pissed off, and will give terrorism a whole new definition."

"That may be so. I don't know how true this is, but I have heard rumors of large groups of your citizens forming militias. Many have died but I hear their numbers are growing."

Chapter 33

Westerly

"Sparrow. Come in."

A few seconds later Brandon's voice returned Mark's excited radio hail. "You've spotted Richard and Amanda's boat?"

"No, that's not why I called you. Jimar was just telling us the Chinese were behind the grid going down."

"No kidding. Not all that surprising though."

"Well, then how about this, the Chinese have landed on the West coast and the Russians on the East. Both are building military bases in order to partition off and lay claim to large portions of the country before some sort of treaty takes effect."

"The radio remained silent for a few minutes as Brandon and Judy let the gravity of the message fully set in."

"Did he say anything about our military?"

"Yeah, he mentioned something, but the news isn't much better. The majority of our troops are stranded in other countries. I guess we were so busy trying to protect other countries from our enemies we ended up not keeping enough troops on the home front to protect the hen house. He did say armed militias are giving them a hard time."

"So how are the troops supposed to get home?"

"According to what Jimar heard, any way they can. I know you two are concerned about meeting up with your son, but it looks like we're going to be traveling down a long road before we have solid..."

The indistinct sound of an excited voice in the background interrupted Mark mid-sentence.

"Jimar thinks the boat he saw with the girl on the helm is sitting off to starboard. I can't tell if it's Richard and Amanda from here but it kind of looks like their boat. I'll try to hail them on the radio."

A sense of relief finding Richard and Amanda fell over the group as Mark cued the mic.

"Hailing Richard and Amanda... Hailing Richard and Amanda... Please respond. Over."

The call was met with silence.

Mark tried hailing the blue hulled boat for a second time as the distance between the boats began to close. Still no response. The movement of one or more people could be seen on the deck.

"Brandon, you copy?"

"Yeah Mark, go ahead."

"We see movement on deck, but it looks like they have no intentions of letting us catch up to them. What do you think?"

"Does it look like Richard and Amanda's boat?"

"The colors look right but all we can really see is the stern. We're going to have to fire up the motor, if we want to catch up to them."

Mark continued to chase after the illusive boat for the next fifteen minutes.

"Brandon, you copy?"

"Go ahead Mark."

"We're catching up to the boat and it's not, I repeat not, Richard's boat."

"What about the girl Jimar said he saw at the helm?"

"Yeah, she's on the helm as we speak."

"Then why isn't she stopping?"

"Well, I'm looking at her with binoculars and I'd say from what I can tell she looks every bit as pretty as Amanda. Yes, in fact I'd say she could pass for Amanda's dark skinned Jamaican twin."

"What do you mean Jamaican twin? Do you think Jimar deliberately lied to us?"

"No, it's not Jimar's fault. We just assumed the girl he saw at the helm that night was white."

"So that's why they're not letting you catch up to them."

"Yeah, they're definitely trying to keep their distance. Maybe they think we're going to try and pull off a pirate...wait."

Two puffs of smoke could be seen emanating from the cockpit of the boat they were chasing followed seconds later by what sounded like two faint pops.

"LuAnn thinks they just took a couple of shots at us. We're not going to stick around for them to target practice on."

"No shit. Get the hell out of range."

"That's an understatement. Listen, we should have found or, at least, heard from Richard and Amanda by now. The longer we hang around this place the scarier it gets."

"I agree. Let's steer a westerly course out of here."

"Nobody can say we didn't give them enough time to meet up with us."

"Yeah, it's a shame they didn't show. We're definitely going to miss them for sure."

Within twenty minutes Mark had caught up and maneuvered his boat a couple of hundred yards downwind of Sparrow. The steady winds created a comfortable sea state for sailing as they distanced themselves from an unfriendly Haitian shoreline.

Judy picked up the mic and casually announced over the radio, "Remind me to put Haiti on the 'be sure to skip' list on the way back."

"The list is starting to grow isn't it?" LuAnn responded.

"It makes you start to wonder what we're doing out here. Brandon and I are starting to re-think our decision to hole up in Panama. Given a choice from what we've had to deal with, we're starting to think we would rather join a militia defending our country than dying in some unexpected storm like Richard and Amanda or being murdered by pirates. Besides, let's face it, do we really want to spend the rest of our lives living out a meaningless life in some dictator driven bullshit country?"

A few seconds later LuAnn came back over the radio. "We've been starting to have the same thoughts."

Judy's voice took on a more serious tone. "The return trip is not going to be a cake walk."

LuAnn agreed while adding, "At least we have a slight advantage on the trip back to Florida."

"What's the advantage?" Judy asked.

"We've learned how to stay alive on limited resources. We're better at recognizing deception, dealing with strangers and discovering a few areas to definitely avoid on the way back."

"Speaking of strangers, what about Jimar?"

The radio went silent for about a minute before LuAnn responded.

"Jimar wants to stay with us. He says he always wanted to see America and with his sister, nephew and brother-in-law dead, he has no living relatives to go back to."

Brandon motioned for Judy to hand him the mic. "Awesome Jimar, I think you've gotta be a little crazy to go back with us but awesome just the same. Besides, we can definitely use another person on our side that can shoot a gun."

Judy took the mic and spoke in a more somber tone, "It's too bad Richard and Amanda won't be making the return trip with us."

LuAnn commented in a thoughtful tone of voice, "Richard would have thought we were crazy turning around and going back."

"I don't think so." Judy said, "I have a feeling Richard and Amanda would have wanted to join us. At least that's the way I'm going to remember them."

Chapter 34

Safe to Say

The tiny two boat fleet methodically worked its way northward toward Florida. Food supplies would be strained to the max over the next two to three weeks. Being unsure of the weather, it would force both boats to adhere to a strict food rationing schedule. Water on the other hand wasn't as big an issue since both boats were equipped with water desalination systems.

There was something exciting, yet peaceful about setting sail for "home". Totally unsure of what they would encounter once reaching familiar waters kept their thoughts continually processing the 'what ifs'. What if there was a blockade at the entrance of Tampa Bay? What if the entire region was under foreign control? The only thing useful about the relentless mental 'what ifs' was taking their minds off the mundane tasks associated with keeping their boats on their north westerly course.

Daily check-in calls became part of the morning routine.

"This is Mark. Day eight since we left Hades. How are you guys doing this beautiful morning?"

"Good morning Mark. You mean Haiti. Looks like we'll be home in another three or four days."

"No, I meant Hades, as in hell and, yes, that's what I came up with too. I'm really surprised we haven't seen other boats, not that I'm complaining. Still we're getting close to home."

"Maybe the Russians have made the coastline a restricted area."

"If the Russians are supposed to be patrolling this region, they're not doing a very good job."

"Maybe the Russians don't care. What kind of damage could a few small sailboats do to their ships anyway? If they ran over us, we'd be lucky to foul their prop."

"You remember the USS Cole attack in Yemen? One tiny boat loaded with 5 or 6 hundred pounds of explosives and boom. One large hole on the port side of the destroyer. It didn't sink but it had to get towed away for repairs. Don't under estimate the power of small boats."

"Well, thanks Brandon. That was quite inspirational. Now I know why we haven't seen any sign of the Russians. They must have heard two small sailboats were headed their way and went into hiding. Yeah, I'll bet they're shaking in their boots as we speak."

The morning was off to a good start. Brandon and Mark had experienced many harrowing moments since the grid had gone down but nothing had managed to put a damper on their sarcastic sense of humor.

"Speaking of things out of place, look in the sky ahead of us. Those dark specks are really moving up there. They have to be military jets. What do you think is going on?"

It took Mark and few minutes to radio back. "Beats the hell out of us but they seem to be flying in some sort of formation out there."

"Think it could be our jets?"

"Hard to tell. They're too far away."

Mark's reply to Brandon's question conveyed a tone of puzzlement and uncertainty.

"No matter whose side they're on they had to have seen us out here."

During the next five minutes, both boats continued to watch the fast moving jets in the sky start circling as additional small black specks suddenly appeared overhead.

Brandon broke the radio silence. "You guys see that?"

"See what? Where?"

"Look straight up. You can still see the white trails in the sky. It looks like a couple of them launched missiles."

"Yeah, wow! You can definitely see the..."

A couple of seconds later, the distinct sound of explosions could be heard as distant popping coming from the direction the missiles had been traveling.

"Let's hope that was our jets firing the rockets."

Within seconds multiple booms unnerved both crews on their tiny sailboats, as the sonic boom of fighter jets flying supersonic hit the surface of the water. Scanning the sky, in the direction the planes were traveling, revealed the first group of dark specks taking evasive action as the battle for air supremacy pit jet against jet. Looking like black gnats through the binoculars it soon became impossible to separate one group from the other.

Three small black plumes successfully struck their intended targets as the jets disappeared. The fight as far as they could tell from the decks of their boats was over in minutes.

Mark's radio broadcast to Brandon and Judy relayed the biggest understatement since leaving Palmetto, "Unless the Chinese and Russians are fighting each other I think it's safe to say the USA is fighting back and, like it or not, we've found ourselves right in the middle of a war."

Chapter 35

Winners and Losers

A moonless night helped conceal their position as Judy and Jimar sailed the two boats a safe distance off the Florida coastline.

The lack of traffic on the return trip up the coast lent to speculation among the group that the worst part of the collapse had passed. Whether through starvation, or occupation, the chaotic waters they had escaped from months earlier would have appeared safe to travel if it were not for the air battle they had witnessed that morning.

The last thing they would have expected was crossing paths that night with a remnant of the air battle.

"That looks like a dim light flickering on and off in the water."

Brandon's statement put Judy on high alert.

"Where? Judy asked. "I'm not going to hit anything am I?"

"No, you're fine. It's off a short distance on the right."

Brandon went below and a few seconds later appeared on deck with a large flashlight. He steadied himself against the cabin trunk as Sparrow rose and fell off the oncoming swells. The bright light illuminated an area off their starboard beam. The faint sound of someone desperately trying to draw their attention was barely audible over the sound of the sea.

"HEY, OVER HERE! I'M OVER HERE!"

Brandon and Judy turned their heads in the direction of the plea half startled to hear a nearby voice emanating from the darkness.

"WHERE ARE YOU?" Judy hollered as Brandon radioed Marks boat that they were about to rescue an unknown voice in the dark.

"You're starting to move past me now! I'm about forty feet off your beam!"

"HOLD TIGHT!" Judy yelled out, "I'll bring us to a stop."

Judy quickly tacked Sparrow into the wind. Without pulling the jib through to the same side of the boat as the mainsail, Sparrow went into a "heave-to" position. They slowly brought the boat to a near stop. Brandon scanned the water with the flashlight trying to locate the exact position of the castaway. Keeping a boat heave-to would enable the person in the water to swim over to the boat, unless he was injured then they could always dinghy over to help him. The condition of the wind and waves that night made it easy for a safe recovery.

As the person in the water swam toward them Brandon was able to make out a single person in the water wearing what appeared to look like a military jump suit.

Brandon secured the boarding ladder near the cockpit. A couple of minutes later he gave a hand helping a young looking pilot climb aboard.

"Were you part of what went on today?"

"Yeah. We've had better days."

"Anyone else get shot down?"

"I don't know. After I got hit I lost track of the other guys."

"I take it you were waiting around for a rescue party?"

"You've got to be kidding. If we go down, we're on our own."

Mark's voice came over the radio, "Is he on board yet?"

"Yes, he's one of the pilots we saw today."

"He's on our side, right?"

"Yep, red, white and blue. I'll get back to you in a couple of minutes."

"Where are you guys going to?" The young stranger asked.

"We were on are way to Panama."

Brandon's reply put a smile on the young pilots face. "Don't take this the wrong way but I think Panama is the other direction."

"Yeah, we know. We were half way there when we decided to change our mind and come back."

"So you're deliberately working your way up the coast?"

"Yeah, something like that."

The young pilot couldn't help but continue to smile. A few minutes later Judy handed the pilot a cup of hot chocolate to help ease his shivering brought on by mild hypothermia.

"Thank you Ma'am."

"Don't thank me, thank you." We have a son in the Air Force a little younger than you."

"Really. Where is he based?"

"Cannon, New Mexico."

"New Mexico. 'No mans' land. They're dealing with the Chinese."

"What do you mean 'no mans' land?"

"It's kind of like the old wild west. The center of the country is too large an area for the Russians and the Chinese to even think trying to control at this stage. Not that they wouldn't love to. They can't afford to commit the resources needed to control all the gun-toting resistance fighters."

"How long do you think we can hold out?"

"Hard to say. I can tell you, thanks to the wars in the Mideast, we learned how effective IED tactics work."

"IED?" Judy asked.

"Improvised Exploding Device."

"You mean like roadside bombs?"

"That and more. Let's just say I think they grossly underestimated American ingenuity with household chemicals."

"Where are you based?" Judy asked.

"Sorry, that's classified. All I can say is we do a good job of keeping them guessing."

"Can you tell us if we're winning?"

"To be honest, I don't really know."

"Why didn't we just nuke the hell out of them?"

"By the time we realized that the grid going down was the start of a carefully, preplanned invasion by the Russians and Chinese it was too late."

"Most of the people lucky enough to survive the looting and killing were rounded up and trucked to FEMA camps. We're talking by conservative estimates 5 million people on the East coast alone. There's no way in hell we were going to drop a nuke on millions of Americans. We had no choice but fight a conventional war."

"What about the West coast?"

"Same story but I haven't heard any estimates. Tell me this, where exactly are you guys sailing to?"

"We were thinking back to the Tampa Bay area. Why?"

"You said you were interested in helping the resistance?"

"Any way we can. Yeah, that's the general plan."

"Can I make a suggestion if you really want to contribute to the cause?"

"Gladly. Shoot."

"Change your course for Rio Bravo Light on the southern Texas border with Mexico."

"Then what?"

"If you follow the Northside of the Rio Grande towards Port Brownsville, you'll be able to join one of the biggest resistance camps fighting for the countries survival and help liberate America."

"Rio Bravo Light?"

"Break out your charts and I'll show you."

Chapter 36

Mach 2

Judy and Brandon continued to devour the wealth of information the young pilot was willing to share. For the first time since leaving Florida they were receiving the most current state of the country.

Exhausted from fighting off the elements as he aimlessly bobbed around for hours in the water, the young pilot went below for much needed rest and quickly fell asleep. Brandon and Judy were embarrassed as they realized in their excitement of catching up on the latest developments, they had failed to ask the pilot what his name was. When he woke from his sleep, they learned his name was Steven. Brandon had a feeling going to the Texas border also had something to do with Steven's ability to reconnect with his airborne unit.

Brandon wasted no time on the radio relaying everything the pilot had said to Mark and LuAnn. A course was quickly plotted as the small group finally had a purposeful destination.

A heading of 263 degrees would have to be maintained for the next seven hundred and ninety miles to reach Rio Bravo Light on the Texas/Mexico border. They were going to have to cross a vast open stretch of the Gulf of Mexico. Having enough food was debatable for a six to seven-day voyage. Decent wind would have to play a major role if they were to make a successful crossing before becoming completely dependent on fishing for food.

The two boats continued to keep each other in sight aided by the blessing of a constant seven to twelve knot breeze the first three days of the voyage. The fourth day found them aimlessly drifting on a sea of glass. Without the steady breeze, the sun and sea enhanced the scene with a dose of stifling humidity.

Brandon teased Judy as the sweat ran down his face, "Tell me why we left San Francisco again.

What was it? O yeah, I remember, it was too cold. That's why we moved to Florida, to escape the cold dry air."

"Bitching about the heat isn't going to help. You were a happy camper to leave for warmer waters as I remember it."

Steven not being familiar with Brandon's sense of humor diplomatically intervened in what he perceived to be an escalating heat induced argument.

"That's why I joined the Air Force and not the Navy. Didn't want to deal with the heat. Love regulating the temperature in my F-35. Never too hot. Never too cold."

"Speaking of Jets, how did they manage to shoot you down?"

"There's only so many missiles you can dodge at the same time."

"So you were seriously outnumbered? We couldn't tell who was who through the binoculars."

"Seven of them. Three of us. We took out four of them before I went down."

"Did they surprise you guys?"

"No, we saw them over a one hundred miles out."

"So you knew you were going to be seriously out gunned?"

"No, we knew they were seriously under skilled."

"Sounds like this wasn't your first encounter."

Whether that information was classified or just modesty on Steven's part the answer would remain his secret.

"The fight didn't seem to last very long."

"I guess that depends on your perspective. From yours it's over in a matter of minutes. From ours, battling at Mach 2, time seems to stand still."

Chapter 37

Coast Guard

The sixth day proved to be a sailor's dream as the breeze began to freshen during the predawn hours. Sparrow, again, moved thru the water with grace and ease, as the miles passed beneath her keel.

A relative and welcomed coolness lifted the spirits, as well as helped distance the previous day's uncomfortable sweltering heat.

"So this is what drives you guys to sailing. I have to admit, next to flying, I could live with this." Steven said as he exited the cabin.

Judy smiled as she responded, "Yes, there is life beyond Mach 2. Do you want to try steering for a while?"

Steven shook his head in agreement and quickly positioned himself at the helm.

"Just remember you pull the tiller handle in the opposite direction you want the boat to point."

Judy took her hand off the tiller letting Steven take full control of the helm.

"You can actually feel the power of the wind through the handle can't you? How fast are we moving?"

Judy looked down at the chart plotter and proudly announced, 6.4 knots.

"It looks and feels like 20 knots. This is amazing."

In Steven's preoccupation with the unique perception of feeling like he was flying through the water, Judy had to remind him to keep the compass on a heading of 263 degrees as he slowly let Sparrow start pointing higher into the wind.

"It's not as easy as it looks is it?"

"You're getting the hang of it. If you start to get into trouble just call for help."

"Your friends in the other boat are keeping up with us. I don't understand. Shouldn't their bigger boat move slower through the water?"

"Not at all. Their boat carries proportionately larger sails to compensate for its size. Mark's boat is faster than ours, if he wants to push it. He's technically under sailing it for us to stay this close together. There's other reasons as well but that's it in a nut shell."

The tranquility was suddenly broken by LuAnn's voice over the radio.

"Heads up. Someone is trailing us on our stern."

Brandon, Judy and Steven instantly turned their heads aft. Brandon handed Judy a pair of binoculars before going below to retrieve a second pair.

"See anything?" Steven asked Judy.

"It's hard to make out."

Brandon handed Steven the binoculars he had brought out on deck knowing his eyesight as a jet fighter pilot, was far superior to his poor vision.

"It's not a sailboat." Judy responded.

"If you look close, it looks like there's another boat behind it. It's just visible to the right."

Steven was right. Brandon quickly informed Mark and his crew there were two boats shadowing them.

A couple of minutes later Mark hailed Sparrow.

"How do you guys want to handle this? In a couple of hours, it's going to be dark. They don't seem to be catching up that fast but they are gaining. Do we want to contact them to find out what their intentions are?"

"That will give us a heads up on options. Go ahead and hail them."

"This is the United States Coast Guard calling the sailboats ahead of us. We just monitored your ship-to-ship communication. Slow to a stop and prepare to be boarded. Do you copy?"

The two boats thinking they were well clear of being heard by transmitting on low VHF radio power were caught with their proverbial pants down.

"That's bullshit." Steven adding, "There is no United States Coast Guard in operation anymore. If they were, they wouldn't be having trouble overtaking us. Nothing the Coast Guard owns moves this slowly."

Once again an unfamiliar voice came over the radio.

"This is the United States Coast Guard. If we have to chase you down, you are going to severely regret it. Failure to stop will result in forcing us to fire on you without further warning. DO YOU COPY?"

The lack of response from the sailboats clearly frustrated the unidentified trailing bandits.

Mark quickly dropped sails and, with the aid of his diesel engine, maneuvered alongside Sparrow.

Hollering over the sound of his engine the two boats quickly discussed a plan of escape.

Chapter 38

Sacrifice

One benefit of a slow boat chase manifested itself in giving them ample time to come up with a workable plan.

Past experience lent itself toward keeping it simple. The fewer components to a plan the less to go wrong. Two boats a hundred miles from shore reinforced that concept since there wasn't an abundance of resources to work with.

Within a short period of time, numerous ideas between them evolved into a workable plan. A plan that wasn't eagerly agreed upon by all. Sacrifices were going to have to be made. Sometimes emotional attachment has to be weighed against the severe penalty of indecision. This was that sometime.

The two boats struggled to maintain as much distance as possible from the slightly gaining pursuing boats that displayed no signs of giving up their prey.

With the help of Mark's crew, Sparrow's life support components, along with Judy and Steven, were transferred to Mark's boat. No easy task on a rolling sea. Lightening Sparrow's load would ensure her sailing as fast as she could in a valiant effort to hold her distance into the dark. Every minute counted as the sun quickly sank below the horizon.

Brandon, the sole occupant, continued to hold Sparrow on as fast a course as she could sail. Buying every minute to distance Sparrow into the darkness was paramount for the plan to succeed.

As darkness fell, Mark gave the order. Brandon turned on Sparrow's electric motor and tied the helm in place. He quickly furled the jibs and let the mainsail halyard loose enabling the large sail to fall to the deck.

Going below he opened a quart size container of barbeque starting fluid and heavily doused the interior cushions. Trying to remain unemotional he lit a match setting her interior on fire.

Pausing before climbing onto Mark's boat, he took one last look at the boat he and Judy had called home and, in a not so weird way, a friend that had given them the ability to distance themselves from danger. Living up to that legacy, she was performing one last defiant act of contributing to their continued survival.

As Sparrow slowly began to burn brighter in the evening sky, Mark set a course ninety degrees away from the direction Sparrow was motoring. The plan was to use her as bait in order to draw the bad guys away from their true position.

The next few hours were tense as all hands on deck constantly scanned the dark night for signs of the intruders. Eventually, showing no indication of being detected, the crew settled into a relieved and relaxed mood.

"Not a bad plan Mark. What made you think of it?" Steven asked.

Mark smiled taking credit, "It just came to me. I guess sometimes I'm just some sort of genius at coming up with original ideas."

Brandon had a harder time dealing with Mark's success at the cost of sacrificing Sparrow. "It was a good plan; I'll give you that but hardly original. As I remember, there was a scene in Captain and Commander where they towed a lit lifeboat behind them to draw enemy fire away from their ship. Like I say, not exactly original Mark, but it worked."

Judy, tired of Mark and Brandon's constant harassing each other blurted out, "I don't care who came up with it. I'm just thankful those guys didn't see the movie."

Everyone laughed in agreement except Jimar who was trying to understand the personalities of the new strangers on board. He would soon realize Brandon and Mark thoroughly enjoyed heckling each other for fun and never held a grudge. It was just their personalities. It did bring out a side of Mark, Jimar hadn't seen before. The same could be said about Steven. He was about to face a thousand questions from LuAnn and Mark. Generally, it sucked to be a new crew person onboard.

Mark's boat now seemed crowded, but the camaraderie definitely outweighed the inconvenience.

Mark and Brandon stood in the companionway and informed the crew they would be nearing Rio Bravo Light tomorrow. Forced to run the diesel yesterday had seriously depleted his fuel supply. Thankfully the wind was strong enough and out of the right direction to enable them to sail. If the wind should die, he estimated the boat had enough fuel left in the tank to make landfall.

Around noon Mark and Brandon, after careful review of the charts, emerged from the cabin to address the crew.

"Listen up. I want to assign each one of you a rifle and a station on the boat. We don't know what it's going to be like going in tomorrow."

Brandon adding, "Best case scenario, we sail close enough to beach the boat and get off. Worst case, we have to fight our way in."

An awkward moment of silence fell over the boat.

Judy spoke up. "So what you're saying is it's either going to be a cake walk or suicide run."

Mark wasn't pleased with the analogy. "We won't know until we get there but, one way or another, we're going in. Look, we're heading for what looks like a deserted stretch of beach if that helps. If anyone has a problem with the plan you're welcome to take the dinghy and strike out on your own. Everyone who agrees with the plan say aye when I call your name."

"Judy", "Aye."

"LuAnn", "Aye."

"Steven", "Aye, aye."

"Jimar..."

"Jimar, Aye or Bye?"

"Jimar says Aye."

"Excellent. Try to get as much rest as you can tonight. I want everyone on top of their game tomorrow."

The remainder of the day was devoted to familiarizing everyone with the weapons they were going to use. Mark and Steven worked with the women showing them how to aim and load the clips before test firing the guns. Anything that would float was thrown overboard to practice on.

Early evening found everyone sitting near or in the cockpit. Steven answered questions about the resistance by stating right up front the information he was passing on was evenly divided between fact and rumors. Before calling it a night he informed the group he would be leaving them when they made landfall to rejoin his squadron.

"I can't reveal how I'm going to reconnect with my squad without jeopardizing our retrieval network. I wish you guys the best when we hit the beach but don't try to follow me."

Chapter 39

Sailing Into Chaos

By midmorning they were an hour away from the great unknown. Any decision to put off the landing until nightfall was dismissed due to Mark's over-evaluation of remaining diesel in the tank. Whether under power or under sail they were going straight in.

"Rio Bravo Light" Brandon announced.

The shoreline was barely visible through the morning haze. Not much more than a flat brown looking streak on the horizon.

"According to the chart plotter we're right on course." Mark said, acknowledging Brandon's sighting.

Steven carefully scanned in the direction they were traveling. "So far so good. I don't see any problem."

"Everyone keep a close watch. We're motoring to the only spot onshore where we have direct access to the mainland."

"I don't understand. It looks like we can beach anywhere we want ahead of us." LuAnn said with a puzzled look on her face.

"Not so." Brandon adding, "Most of the land to the north of the light has a large body of water on the other side."

"So where we're going is attached to the mainland?"

"Exactly. No water or bridges to cross over."

Mark tried to inspire confidence in the proposed landing. "The best way to mentally handle running into trouble is to think of yourselves as already dead. Then you'll have nothing to lose."

Mark has his inspirational moments, but this wasn't one of them.

Brandon tried to lighten the moment. "You're starting to scare us Mark. Do you have anything below I can make a white flag out of? You know, in case we have to surrender to a bunch of angry Mexican peasants for littering the beach with your boat."

Mark's sense of humor remained on hold. Brandon regretted making light of what very well could end in a life or death struggle.

Judy turned to LuAnn and whispered, "Have you noticed how time seems to slow down as the suspense builds."

"I don't know about slowing down. I just want us to get off this fricking boat and find a civilized group of people to live with. Look at all the crap we've had to deal with. I'm tired of running across assholes with no conscience or compassion for other people. They're either trying to kill, steal or rape you."

Twenty minutes later Jimar dashed any hopes of an uneventful landing. "Here comes trouble." He pointed slightly off the port side bow.

Within minutes three low profile speeding boats from the mainland were bearing down on an intercept course.

"Everyone down below. Make sure your gun is cocked and the safety is off."

Jimar went below deck to open the v-berth hatch. Standing on the bed below the hatch with just his head and shoulders exposed on deck resembled a hatch cover on the turret on a tank.

LuAnn, Judy, Brandon and Steven took up position below deck at the open ports in the main salon. They stood ready to fire with their rifles protruding through the ports. Mark remained at the helm, staying as low as possible.

"Wait for my order to fire!" Mark commanded as he aimed straight for the middle of the oncoming boats.

If anything remotely had a calming effect, it was the muffled sound of Mark's diesel engine running flat out. The rhythmic vibration of the pistons surged through the boat. As long as you could feel and hear the engine making way for the shore meant you were still alive.

The victor of this water borne battlefield wasn't going to be decided by 'right or wrong', 'good versus evil' or 'might makes right'. It was going to be decided by determination. One side hell bent on domination, the other, freedom.

As the speeding boats closed in on their intended victim, Mark could see tiny splashes hitting the water ahead of them. The attacking boats had started firing well out of range of doing any damage.

Over the sound of the motor, the crew below could hear Mark defiantly yell, "If you think you're going to scare us into stopping by rattling off a few shots, you assholes are in for a little surprise!"

Showing no signs of backing down from their threat, the gunfire intensified. Mark, crouching as low as he could get while still enabling himself to steer continued to pilot his boat toward the shore. Thirty-seconds later the sound of bullets striking fiberglass signaled the enemy was in range. Mark gave the order for the crew open fire.

The sound of semi-automatic gunfire emanating from the forty-foot sailboat sounded like orchestrated mayhem. The speeding boats broke formation, wildly shooting as they passed, two to starboard and one to port. Each boat carried three men onboard, two gunmen and a driver. All the men appeared to be dark skinned which leaned toward the assailants being Mexican nationals.

The cabin trunk on Mark's boat afforded little protection from the oncoming barrage. The four small 8X16 inch ports in the main salon did however give everyone inside the boat an illusion of protection by concealing their exact firing position inside the boat.

Having weathered the first assault, the boats regrouped a short distance off before remounting a second attack. Having sized up their opposition they approached Mark's boat this time from the rear. One boat on the starboard side and two on Mark's port. Bullets randomly began to hit both sides of the boat as they roared by. The return fire from the interior of the sailboat was deafening. Judy suddenly slumped back motionless. One of the shots fired in her direction had found its target.

"Judy's hit!" Brandon hollered as the gunmen continued their attack.

"How bad?" LuAnn asked, barely able to take her eyes off the menacing boats as they sped past her position.

"She's not moving. I don't think she's breathing," he said.

Steven in a voice meant to shock Brandon back into the fight hollered, "Brandon, cover your side, we can't help her now. If we don't kill these fuckers, we're all going to die."

The port side attacker misjudged the speed of its lumbering prey. The driver suddenly made an attempt to cut in front of Mark's boat. Jimar instantly took advantage of his forward position to unleash a short burst of bullets killing the driver. The pilotless boat turned in front of Mark's boat and within seconds the horrific sound of crunching fiberglass ensued as the beam of the small boat was violently rammed and forced out of the way. The impact flipped the boat on its side injuring the two gunmen and throwing them into the sea.

The two remaining boats must have been communicating with each other over walkie-talkies as they simultaneously turned and circled a safe distance from Mark's boat. As if on cue, they both executed a semicircle path thru the water in opposite directions to approach Mark's boat head-on from both sides. It instantly became obvious they were speeding straight for the middle of the fleeing sailboat.

With guns spitting out a flurry of rounds, the enemy had managed to minimize their profile while delivering a potentially lethal barrage of bullets in the direction of the shooters concealed within the sailboats midsection.

The plan might have succeeded except for the fact the small boats were hobby horsing so bad through the water it was next to impossible for the gunmen to accurately hit where they were aiming.

"Wait till they turn and give'em hell!" Mark yelled.

Mark was right. At some point the gunboats were going to have to break off the attack in order to avoid colliding with his boat.

Fifty feet from impact, they started an evasive escape maneuver by angling toward the rear of the sailboat.

With Judy out of the fight the starboard defense of the boat fell solely on Brandon and Jimar's shoulders.

Over the sound of gunfire, they could hear Mark holler, "Damn it."

Steven quickly turned to look outside at the helm as Mark who had crouched as low as he could in the cockpit continued to steer toward the shore. "You all right?"

Having to yell over the sound of the diesel Mark hollered back, "Yeah, I'm okay. I didn't even realize I got hit." A slow but steady flow of blood could be seen running down Mark's left arm.

Whether it came from the barrel of Brandon or Jimar's rifle, they could visibly see one of the port side gunmen slump forward and remain motionless. LuAnn and Steven continued to target their nemesis.

A strange calm suddenly fell over the water. Bobbing safely out of range the remaining gunmen were probably deciding whether further loss of life on their part was worth whatever treasure the sailboat might or might not be carrying.

Mark watch as the gunmen sped away. He slowly stood up and calmly announced, "We won. They're heading away."

As quickly as it had started, it was over.

Brandon backed away from his gun station and quietly sat next to Judy's lifeless body.

"Nice shooting you guys." Steven said as LuAnn tore a strip from a galley towel to wrap around Mark's wound. "Everyone else okay?"

Brandon understandably didn't answer back.

"Jimar, how are you doing up front? Jimar?"

Not hearing a reply Steven instantly made his way forward toward the v-berth where he found Jimar still wedged in the hatch cover opening.

Mark and LuAnn listened intently as Steven broke the news, "Jimar didn't make it either."

Chapter 40

Farewells

As the attacking boats slowly faded into the hazy horizon, the aftermath of what had just taken place slowly and sadly sunk in.

Judy and Jimar were victims of circumstance. Their destiny put into motion months earlier with the collapse of a civil society and spawned by violence.

LuAnn hugged Brandon who openly wept at the loss of his wife, assuring him they would give Judy and Jimar a proper funeral onshore.

Mark slowly and gently made landfall beaching his bullet riddled boat in five feet of water. Guns and food were quickly removed from the boat. The remaining survivors gently lowered Judy and Jimar's bodies into the dinghy for the short transport to shore.

An hour after making landfall Steven and Mark dug two shallow graves well out of the water's reach. Their bodies were wrapped in sailcloth cut from the boat's Genoa sail.

"Judy loved to sail. I think she would have approved of being buried in sailcloth."

"I agree. She really seemed to love sailing didn't she. I feel bad for Jimar too. He was really looking forward to seeing America." Mark said.

A few words were said over their shallow resting place. Mark volunteered to cover up the graves as Brandon sat a short distance from the gravesites staring out to sea.

"It's going to take a long time for him to get over Judy's death." LuAnn said to Mark, adding, "Just goes to show you how fragile and fleeting an existence we live."

Steven recommended they quickly leave the area and follow the river until they make contact with the local resistance fighters.

"I'm sorry for your loss." He then turned to face Brandon. "I can't thank you enough for plucking me out of the water."

Brandon extended his hand to shake. "So this is it. You're going to head out and find your outfit."

"Yes, it'll take me a while but I'll get back."

"I wish you good luck and good hunting in the sky."

"The same goes for the three of you locating the resistance."

Steven then shook Mark's hand and LuAnn gave him a big hug and wished him a safe journey.

Brandon, Mark and LuAnn, the last surviving members of the original nine people that left Palmetto picked up their supplies, shouldered their weapons and began walking toward an unsure future.

About the Author

Larry Dodson recently relocated from northern California to the warm seaside community of Palmetto, Florida. Having an extensive sailing background over the last forty years as well as a belief in being self-sufficient in the event of a nationwide catastrophe served to inspire his first book "Destination Unknown: A Desperate Tale Of Survival".

Made in the USA
Lexington, KY
20 May 2017